More titles by Judy Garwood

No Loose Ends
A Lady Kate Mystery

Original Louisiana Folk Art Paintings by Ray Taix.

Kate is the only granddaughter of The Duke of Devon, Lord and Lady Sanford. When Kate is in England she's Lady Kate and when in the Louisiana bayou, she's Private Investigator Kate Bodine.

She trained in aiki-ju-jutsu, karate, and judo, for six years, earning a second degree black belt in each art. While in graduate school, she took private lessons in "real world application" under her sensei.

During that time she also became an excellent marksman.

Kate Bodine is hired by Mike Greenwald, successful start-up computer company owner, to find Diana Dorsey, a woman he fell in love with, who disappeared in Cornwall, England.

Diana was on her way to join him in Connecticut when she vanished. Mike stopped trying to find her until he receives a postcard from her saying, "Help Me."

My overwhelming thanks to Hanshi Tony Annesi who has not only been editor for my past books but he wrote all the Martial Arts action scenes in the first of the Lady Kate Mysteries, "No Loose Ends." Hanshi Annesi is a 9th Degree black belt and has taught Martial Arts for over 50 years (www.bushido-kai.net). His fiction includes *1969: Loss of Innocence* and *The Shangrilla Artifacts* trilogy.

Ray Taix hand drew the cover and back for two of my books and used his photos for two others. Ray is an award-winning artist. (ray@ thebrotherstaix.com)

Agostino de Noia, a DEA police agent in Italy, is my reference for all drug and police questions.

Ray Lota fixed my writing desk, desk chair, and my computer. What would a writer do without those necessities? (proassist1999@gmail. com)

To my son, Ben Garwood,

whose support has been unwavering

Judy Garwood

No Loose Ends

A Lady Kate Mystery

PROLOGUE

The pirogue cut through the murky waters of the bayou. Gnarled cypress trees stood like observant sentinels, knee deep in the dark waters. Spanish moss, delicately laced through dead and rotting branches, hung down, stretching towards a watery grave. The air was thick with moisture.

A man stood poised in the pirogue. Sinewy muscles flexed under his blue work shirt as he sunk a long pole deep into the rotting vegetation at the bottom of the canal waterway. He leaned heavily against it. The canoe shot forward. He repeated the motion over and over again. Only the water lapping at the sides of the narrow boat testified to the intrusion.

Fireflies flickered and played in the trees lining the bank. Reaching his destination the man pulled the pole out of the water and allowed the pirogue to drift to a stop. Fumbling with a match, he lit the wick on a lantern and hung it on a pole trailing over the water behind him. It cast a golden glow over the surrounding area.

Reaching down into a tarnished metal bucket, he pulled out

a fistful of animal parts. Long ropes of bloody entrails whipped like frenzied snakes over the waters as the man spread out the feast. He didn't dare wash his hands in the water. He wiped them off on his pants.

Within minutes, lured by the scent of blood, dozens of short-snouted creatures with unblinking eyes slithered off banks, submerged, reappeared and gobbled up the offering.

The man grinned. Bending over he pulled away a canvas cover that had hidden its secret in the bottom of the canoe.

Easily, for one born on the bayou, the man maintained his balance on the pirogue while he slid his burden over the side. A furious commotion in the dark water followed. The man laughed as he watched.

Unnoticed, a floppy brimmed, brown felt hat sloshed around in the bottom of the boat before secreting itself away under a wedge of wood in the stern.

Satisfied, the man skillfully turned the pirogue around and returned the way he had come.

ONE

"Okay, I'm going to go through this just one more time. Best guess is the Mayor." She tried to read the agent's blank expression.

"Because it's his house? You know how crazy that sounds?" Jack Sullivan ran his hand through his dark straight hair.

She dropped a pair of torn underwear back on the bed. "Hey, you guys brought me in on this. I didn't ask for it." She sighed. "I call it like I see it. I know you all were hoping it was the gardener, or the housekeeper, or the butler but it wasn't since no staff is ever in residence when the Governor visits. And yes, it's the Mayor's house. Security inside and out is so tight a mosquito couldn't make a fly by." Today was a good day, she thought, because sometimes things made sense, sometimes they didn't. She had no idea where the crazy idea that she had the magic touch and could go back in time seeing where something had been but it too much energy to dispel the myth. Let them think what they wanted. In this case the Governor always stayed at the the Boudreaux House, the Mayor's 18th century mansion in the French Quarter when he visited. She knew there were secret passageways that connected many of the rooms. And the passageways in the Mayor's house were made for slaves with small bodies. The

Mayor happened to have a very small frame. Put two and two together, she thought. She paused since there was no reaction to what she was saying. "You see the Mayor sneaks---"

"Okay, okay. I got the picture." Jack paced back and forth. "I don't know how I'm going to tell Governor Charles that every time he visits New Orleans the Mayor, sight unseen and bypassing all security, goes into the Governor's bedroom and takes a pair of scissors to his wife's uh...undergarments!"

"I've got an idea. Why don't you suggest the Governor not stay in the Boudreaux house?" She grinned and shook her head. "I can't believe they brought the FBI in on this case."

"Mrs. Charles has been a nervous wreck." He paced back and forth.

"Yeah, and to say nothing about how much fun it must be for a sixty year old woman to go to a political dinner without any underwear."

Jack groaned. Kate Bodine smiled as she shrugged into a navy gabardine wool blazer.

Jack gave her a speculative look. She was the prettiest Private Investigator he'd ever seen. Long blonde hair, dark grey eyes, a rosy English complexion. Jack liked her when they first met a few years ago. At the time he made it his business to check her out. But, at the time, with Peter Edwards in the picture there was no chance. Jack knew her mother was from England and her father was a Cajun born in White

Castle, Louisiana. They met while her Father was on loan to Scotland

Yard from the New Orleans Police Department. It was love at first sight

and they married in a grand ceremony befitting the only daughter of a

Duke and his wife, Lady Cathryn.

Kate was born one year later and spent the first twelve years of

her life living, with her parents in Greystone Abbey, the family estate on

the Cornish coast. Her mother died in a tragic horse jumping accident

when Kate was twelve years old. Missing his family Jock Bodine

brought Kate back to Louisiana three years later which was a huge blow

to her mother's family. They had grown close to Jock and they loved

Kate. And Kate dearly loved them. It was a fact that she flew back to

see her grandparents more than a few times a year.

Jack knew that after college and grad school, in Boston, she

joined the New Orleans Police Department. It was in the family. Her

father and three of his brothers were working rank. Kate had met the

love of her life in college. Peter Edwards was a military sniper and an

instructor in the Army Marksmanship Unit after he graduated. He

followed her to New Orleans and joined the Police Force.   They made

plans to quit the Police Force, get married and start their own security

business but he was killed in a routine traffic stop. He died instantly.

Kate was devastated and quit the NOPD. Following their dream she

became a freelance security advisor but to pay the bills she also got a

License as a Private Investigator. Peter had taught her marksmanship.

It was said she was better than most snipers. During her six years in Massachusetts she studied martial arts at Bushido-kai dojo in Framingham, earning a second degree black belt in aki-ju-jutsu, karate and judo. Kate was a natural.

New Orleans is a town where what counts is who you know and who your contacts are. And Kate knew a lot of people. They call her in when they have a case that requires insight into the mind of a serial killer or serial rapist. She is thirty years old and single. Her work keeps her busy in New Orleans. But when she has any free time she escapes to the peace and quiet of her houseboat in Bayou Savage. She calls Big Fred, who hangs out on the front porch, a security guard who works for raw chicken parts. Big Fred just happens to be a mean, lean, ten-foot alligator that hisses like crazy when anyone but Kate approaches. She loves the bayou but most of the time you can find her in her office/apartment in the French Quarter. The intriguing thing about Kate Bodine is that she uses common sense to figure things out. She had breezed in, cool as could be, draped her navy blazer over the back of a chair and went to work. Grabbing a handful of shredded panties she had slumped down in a comfy leather armchair and gone into a deep meditation. When she returned to a conscious state she had one hell of a story to tell. The Mayor no less! Jack didn't want to look stupid when he explained to a room full of other agents just who the unsub was. "Hey, Kate, just what is it you do?"

"Now that's a stupid question." Kate looked up from the paperwork she had to fill out. "If the FBI doesn't know, who does?

What's with you guys? Do you go to school to learn how to ask questions like that or does it just come naturally?" She stood, dropping the papers on the table and grinned at him. "I'm a Private Investigator."

"I meant the going into the trance thing and coming up with an answer. Humor me. Tell me how does the Mayor get past our agents in the hallway?"

"And the ones outside? And even places you can't see!" Kate rolled her eyes. She knew about the secret passageways because when her Dad brought her back to New Orleans, after her Mum died, they lived in a two hundred year old house in the Quarter. She quickly found out about the secret passages and how to get around unseen. The pirate, Jean Lafitte, had smuggled contraband in and out that way. A latch was usually hidden inside the fireplace. She went over, reached in, and pushed a recessed area in a firebrick, not visible to the naked eye. A small, concealed door in the walnut paneled room silently slid open.

"You're good." Jack smiled.

Kate grinned. He might not be able to find a secret door but he sure was cute. She had seen him around. She checked his ring finger. He was still single, she thought. A pain touched her heart when she thought about Peter but she had decided to go forward with her life. Peter had been killed over two years ago.

"Hey Kate, how about dinner sometime?"

"Maybe. Give me your number."

Jack wrote his cell on the back of a standard government issue

FBI card and handed it to her.

Kate slipped it into the pocket of her jacket. A navy blazer, faded blue jeans and a white blouse was a kind of uniform for Kate. But when the occasion called for it she had a closet full of ball gowns.

TWO

Kate knew Jack was watching her as she left the room.

A carriage clicked by on the cobblestone streets with a tinkle of bells and the heavy aroma of leather braces. The travel brochures say The French Quarter is the closest a tourist can come to a European village, outside of Europe. She checked her watch. It was almost five o'clock. Where had the time gone?

A cell phone rang in her pocket. She checked the number, not one she recognized. "Hello."

"Kate Bodine?" A male voice inquired.

"You got her. What can I do for you?"

"I want to find someone. I was told you're the best."

Kate sat down on a concrete stoop in front of a row house, typical in the French Quarter. "How much information do you want?"

"Everything."

"Okay?" She had a little bit of a question in her voice.

"Money is no problem. I want to start now."

"Let's meet at my office and we'll talk."

"Good."

"317 Gov Nichols, Apartment 1A. Between Bourbon and Royal. Enter by the open French doors."

"I'll find it."

She checked the time. "How about one hour?"

"See you then and Miss Bodine...thank you."

Smiling, she could just bet his problem was about a woman. What kind of woman would cause a man to spend big bucks to find her? A man in love.

She headed to her office, stopping only for a bowl of chicken gumbo at The Gumbo Shop.

On a peaceful street stood a thirty-foot wide red brick apartment building. A heavily carved mahogany front door opened onto a shared hallway. There was a staircase on the right leading to an identical apartment on each of the upper two floors.

She collected her mail from the aged wall mailbox located in the entryway.

1A, downstairs, first door on the left was home sweet home. Kate walked into a small living room she had converted into an efficient office, with French doors facing Gov Nichols. Cypress pocket doors led through to a breakfast nook, a small kitchen, a bath, and finally her bedroom with floor to ceiling windows that opened onto a charming, private brick courtyard filled with banana trees, giant elephant ears, a variety of ferns and a small, antique copper fountain. She glanced at the Brown and Jordan chaise lounge chair where she spent many hours reading. Her apartment was the only one with access to the courtyard.

She pushed open the French doors, flipped on a large crystal chandelier, fourteen feet overhead, and tossed her mail on an antique desk she had inherited when the guy on the second floor moved out two years ago.

Laying her jacket over the back of a burgundy leather recliner in the corner, she thought about her new client. Money was no object, he said.

Exactly at 6:00 PM there was a knock on the French doors. Her new client was right on time.

THREE

He was the kind of man who looked at ease anywhere. Over six foot tall, slim, he had that confident look that went with being successful. He wore a dark blue Brioni that fit him perfectly. He quickly took in her small, but comfortably furnished, office.

"Mike Greenwald." They shook hands. He sat in the aged cognac leather wing chair across from her desk.

Where had she heard that name before? "What can I do for you, Mr. Greenwald?"

"I want to find someone who is very important to me."

From the Rolex to the Bally shoes he looked like a man who had enough money to locate anyone he wanted. "Why don't you start at the beginning?"

"Last year I was in England for a few months. I fell in love with an American girl, Diana Dorsey, who was living in Penzance, a small village on the Cornish Coast. At the time she was working at the Blue Iron Pub. I had to return to New York. I begged her to come with me. She promised she would organize her personal life and follow in one month. I didn't have the choice of waiting there for her. I'm not a man who falls in or out of love easily. Since then I've tried to find her... nothing."

"Maybe she met someone. Something else might have intervened. Are you prepared for what I might find?"

"For the past week I've been in New Orleans on business. My secretary sent this to me." He handed Kate an envelope with a handwritten postcard inside, no return address. The note said, "Help me! You are the only person I can trust. Dee."

"And this is her handwriting?"

"Yes. But more important is how she signed her note. We used nicknames we made up. She was Dee for Diana. I was Mick. No one would know that but Diana." He paused then handed her a very thin blue file. "Diana sent the note to the last address she had for me a year ago. I was living in Cornwall, Connecticut. When we met she said it was fate since we met in Cornwall in England.

Kate pulled out the one page, turning it over and back. She gave him a questioning look.

"We were having fun." He ran his hand through sandy blonde hair and shifted in his chair. "She didn't talk about her past. And I didn't pry. I thought she'd tell me when she was ready."

Kate returned the page to the file and placed it in front of her. "There might be something in one of the pictures." She almost added, I hope.

"When can you leave for England? The sooner the better."

Kate loved England and the timing was perfect. Her Grandfather had died a year ago. She had reluctantly left after staying with her Granny for one month. After this case maybe she could spend more time with Granny.

"I checked. I know what you charge." Mike handed her a check for twenty thousand dollars "Twenty thousand to start. I'll pay you a thousand dollars a day, all expenses and a twenty thousand bonus when you find her. Does that cover it?" He quickly wrote a number on the back of a business card. "You can leave a message on that number. I'm the only one who answers it." He handed the card to her. In small letters it read The Omega Corporation.

Kate quickly scanned his business card. The Omega Corporation! That explained it. Of course, now she remembered where she had heard his name. It had been all over the news. Mike Greenwald had started the Omega Computer Network and sold it for a huge sum. "This is far more than my usual rate."

"I know." Mike gave her a very direct look. "Like I said, money is no object. Just find Diana. I know she's in trouble."

"Trust me, Mr. Greenwald, if Diana Dorsey can be found, I'll find her. And I'll provide you with a written diary covering every move she's made from the time you left her in Cornwall until now."

"Good. I knew I made the right choice. Call me...anytime."

They shook hands and he left.

Kate put the check in a secret drawer in the desk. She called to make a plane reservation from New Orleans to London. She was leaving at ten the next morning.

FOUR

He was aware of her the minute he entered the tavern. Small town, small town bars...they were the same everywhere. And Bayou Poche was definitely small town. Ed's Diner looked like the only passably good place to eat in town. Layers of smoke hung in the air. Pinesol and urine wafted from the back corner near the bathrooms. Fake fighting erupted from some underage kids near the front door, close to the jukebox. Shrill, pubescent laughter drifted from one barely drinking age group to the next.

Carla discreetly tracked his smooth move from the entrance door to a dark booth in the back near the rear exit. He was older than the regular town guys. She took in his tight jeans, black t-shirt, and well-used leather jacket. He looked like an actor with his blonde streaked hair and strong physique.

She delivered four sodas to a booth filled with rocking teenagers. Leaving the tray on a vacant table she quickly made her way to his booth.

"Hi. What can I get you?" She brushed her long, dark red hair over her shoulder and made sure her breasts were as out there as they were going to get. She would love to take this one home with her. It was the strangers, they were the safe ones. If it was a local or one of the University crowd from the big town next door then word might get around, but with a stranger no one would know what she was doing in the privacy of her own home. Her body ached with excitement. It had been a long time. Too long.

"What's good?"He knew she was looking him over. They were all the same.

"Everything. Don't you know we're the best joint in town... course we're also the only joint in town!" She loved that joke. She hardly ever had the chance except when someone new came in. And that was not often enough, that's for sure. This must be her lucky night.

"You're right, Carla." He smiled at her. There was no chase anymore. It was too easy.

When he smiled she could see he had even, perfect teeth. She brought a hand to her mouth to hide her crooked teeth. She always meant to get them fixed. His eyes were dark blue in the bright light streaming from the suddenly open bathroom door nearby, the color of brand new denim navy jeans. She liked men with blue eyes. Her fingers itched to push the silky blonde hair off his forehead.

"Now how did..." Before she had a chance to get it out he was pointing to her name tag. Wow, or course, he probably thought she was some dummy. She grinned."Sure and yours?"

"Zack." It wasn't his real name but just as good as any other. He pulled his baseball cap over his forehead.

An elderly couple walked in and sat down at a booth in the front.

"Oh, no."She nodded her head in their direction. "Those old folks are really fussy about ordering. Take your time, Zack. I'll be back." She hoped she had made that sound like an invitation. She made sure her back was to the rest of the restaurant patrons. This was personal. She swept her eyes over him starting at his long, muscular legs. When she got to his mouth she licked her lips. She liked the way he discreetly smiled when she did that. Wait until she showed him what she could do with her mouth. The way he was eating her up with his eyes made her tingle all over. She turned away before she jumped into his lap right here in front of everyone.

He didn't have to turn around to know that she wiggled her hips when she walked away. Yeah, he'd score tonight. He'd score and more. He could feel himself losing that tight control he maintained all the time so he concentrated on the home-style menu in front of him.

He was still involved with the menu when she returned.

"I'll have a burger dressed and lots of napkins." He handed her the menu, making sure his hand touched hers.

Carla blushed. "Good choice, Zack." She meticulously wrote down his order on a thick pad.

"You know you have a great body." He stared openly at her

breasts.

His eyes were like hot hands caressing her. Carla blinked from behind her thick glasses.

"Well, thank you!"

"I'm just passing through town. Do you know anywhere I can spend the night?"

Carla made a quick decision. No one was watching them. "How about Chez Moi?"

A slow smile came across his face. "And where would that be?"

"I'll get the directions to you. I get off in half an hour."

"Perfect. I'm good at following directions."

The look he gave her conveyed just what he meant.

She got hot all over. Tonight was going to be a night she'd never forget.

When she returned ten minutes later with his burger she slipped a piece of paper with very specific directions to her cottage.

He carefully wrapped the burger in two or three napkins and ate it that way. When he finished he casually pocketed the napkins. Not a good idea leaving DNA around. He made sure the few things he touched he wiped clean of his fingerprints before he left. He wasn't on anyone's radar but just in case. You can never be too careful, he thought. It was the thing that let him pursue his "hobby" unchecked for the past twenty years.

Finishing his meal he left the café without glancing in her

direction.

She watched him walk out and prayed he'd be at her back door when she got home.

She counted the minutes until her shift was over. She hurried to her car and raced the few blocks to her vine-covered cottage. There was no car in front of her house. She quickly opened the front door and entered the dark living room. Turning on the lights she drew the heavy drapes tightly closed. She didn't want anyone to see her entertaining a gentleman caller. The neighbors were terrible gossips.

She went through the kitchen and opened the back door. He was waiting for her. For just a second he looked menacing as he walked past her into the dark kitchen. She shook off the feeling. He was a stranger, but so what, she liked strangers. They were anonymous. And the sex was the best. She smiled and thought no one would know. She had never been nor did she ever want to be the topic of gossip in town. Unfortunately she was the subject of the only gossip in town the next day. They found her lifeless body in a tub full of water and bleach.

FIVE

He was miles away and it was raining hard when he drove through the town he'd grown up in. He noticed a new bookstore, Sarah's Books, on Main Street. He watched a young woman come out and stand in the doorway deciding what to do next. He knew her. Her name was Sarah something. They had gone to school together. He pulled his Jeep to the curb and got out. The young woman turned and peered through the curtain of rain. Recognizing him she beckoned for him to come in.

"Why Jimmy Landry, I can't believe you're back home. I haven't seen you in what...ten years?" She was breathless when she got a close up look at him. Wow! He looked like a movie star. Age had certainly been good to him.

He grinned and followed her into the warm bookstore.

They had a pleasant time inside her cozy, little shop. She made coffee. They laughed about old times. Then she got close to him, rubbing against him. Did she think he was a fool? He knew what she wanted. It was what they all wanted. It was too easy. But this was his hometown and Sarah was an old school friend. He was very careful about his victims. He never made a mistake. That's why he was still free to do as he pleased. It was the little details that got you in the end.

He made sure to leave no loose ends. Ever.

About an hour, after reminiscing about old times, he pulled on

his black leather driving gloves, handed her two concert tickets and

told her to have a good time. She put them down on an end table with

a framed picture of Sarah standing next to a knockout gorgeous blonde.

"Is that your sister?" He pointed to the girl in the photo with

Sarah.

"On no, that's my cousin."

He waved goodbye to Sarah, got in his Jeep and headed for

New Orleans. The city was right in the middle of the craziness of

Mardi Gras. A perfect place, he thought, to find a naive young girl on

vacation anywhere from California to Maine. He wouldn't have any

problem finding just the right one.

SIX

Kate's cell phone rang. She had to get up early the next morning for the ten o'clock flight to London. She checked her caller ID. It was Aunt Jenny. She never called later at nine at night.

Kate answered and sensed the confusion in her Aunt's voice.

"Katie, dear, I'm so glad to talk to you. I didn't want to bother you at first but now I just don't know what to do."

"Aunt Jenny, is Uncle Johnny okay?"

" Oh yes, he's just fine. Well, I certainly think so. It's not your Uncle Johnny that I'm worried about...it's just...well, dear, I know I'm being overly protective but well...it's just that I'm used to everyone being where they say they're going to be and she isn't."

Aunt Jenny had an endearing quality of just not quite getting to the point. "Who's not where?"

"It's Sarah. I'm worried about her. She's missing. I went over to her house. She just recently moved into the old Victorian on Main Street that she's been fixing up. The one behind her new bookstore but she wasn't there. In fact her bed hasn't even been slept in." Never

married, Aunt Jenny took over the role of mother when, Gloria, Sarah's

mom died. Gloria had been Aunt Jenny's best friend. She had been

married to Gio, Jenny's youngest brother. Gio left Cross Creek and

joined the Police Force in New Orleans, working with his brothers, Jock

and Johnny.

"Have you called everyone?"

"I called you first."

"Please don't worry. I'll take care of everything."

"Maybe I should call Uncle Johnny."

"Don't call him yet. Wait until I get there. Meet me in front of

the bookstore. But don't go in. It's nine o'clock now. I'll be there in one

hour."

Kate thought about her dad's oldest brother, Johnny Bodine,

at home in a wheelchair. Ten years ago Johnny and his wife were in

an automobile accident. His wife died instantly. Depression kept

Johnny in a wheelchair. There was little anyone could do about it. He

had his Police retirement, his brothers, his friends, and being so close

to his sister was a blessing. Aunt Jenny was always running over with

casseroles, driving him to doctor appointments, the grocery and the

pharmacy for his prescriptions.

"Maybe Sarah went off with one of her friends and forgot to

lock up. See you soon, Aunt Jenny."

Disconnecting her cell phone, she slipped it into an inner

pocket of her jacket.

One bad thing about the French Quarter, there is never
anywhere to park on the street. She located her restored 1973 series III
Land Rover, turquoise with a white top. It was a good off road vehicle
but only four cylinders. Kate smiled. Not the fastest car on the road
but definitely very reliable, a quality she liked in a car, and wished she
could find in a man. She started up the engine and headed towards
Cross Creek, Louisiana.

An image of Sarah came into her mind. She was the youngest
of three children. Her cousin grew up and never left the small town of
Cross Creek. Sarah's sister and brother had gotten their mom's delicate
and refined features while Sarah had inherited the course looks of her
dad. She had medium length brown hair and brown eyes. From what
Kate was told Sarah's dream was to open a bookstore and she worked
hard to make it a reality. Working seven days a week and taking a night
job she saved up enough to get a down payment on a boutique that she
converted into her bookstore with a lovely Victorian house connected
to it. What she lacked in start up money the Cross Creek Bank & Trust
took care of. It didn't hurt to have a brother who was the president of
the largest bank in town.

It was exactly ten o'clock when Kate exited the freeway onto
State Route 206. No moon, no street lights. It was black outside. A
heavy, cold rain came down like a curtain.

As she turned onto Main Street, her headlights barely

penetrated a thick fog bank, making it almost impossible to see beyond the hood of the car. She drove carefully. The town had changed very little since the last time she'd visited her cousin.

It was easy to find "Sarah's Books." A little metal sign was hanging from swaying chains much like you'd expect to find at a little pub deep in the English countryside. Not at all something you would think to see in a small Louisiana bayou town, a little over thirty miles west of New Orleans.

Aunt Jenny was nervously waiting in her car when Kate arrived and parked beside her. She quickly got out, giving her beloved aunt a big hug.

She felt her aunt's frail body tremble as she returned the hug. "It might not be anything. Wait here."Kate didn't want her aunt more upset than she already was so she helped her back into the heated car.

The minute Kate touched the front door of the store she felt a sensation of cold quiet. The silence was overwhelming. The smell of new furniture penetrated every nook and cranny. Her hand rested on a small end table beside the couch. A single rock concert ticket, that was taking place in Baton Rouge that evening, lay on the table. If she was putting a bet on it she'd say there had been two but she had only used one.

She hurried outside to talk to her aunt, giving her a reassuring smile.

"Could she have just taken a break? A concert perhaps that she didn't tell you about?"

"No, dear, Sarah is not like that. She would have called me first."

"Aunt Jenny, I think she's gone to a concert. She might be alone. Someone gave her two tickets. One was left on the table unused. She's out having fun. You'll see."

"Okay. Thank you, dear."

She hugged her aunt. "I can't do much more. Unless the local authorities call me in on a case, if there is one, I can't just stick my nose in. You know what I mean? Small town police departments are very small town. In this case I don't think there is anything to worry about."

"I so appreciate your driving in this terrible weather to come and help me."

"I have a big case. I'm going out of town tomorrow but nothing is more important than family to me. If you need me just call."

"Thank you, dear."

Hugging her aunt one last time she left. There was nothing she could do at the moment. Sarah would come home with an exciting adventure story.

Driving back to New Orleans in the pouring rain she thought about her Granny in England. Kate remembered her Grandfather's funeral a year ago and returned every chance she could. Then, as always, it was hard leaving her Granny even if she did have more than enough staff to watch out for her. Kate had grown up living in the west wing of the large palatial estate with her Mum and Dad. Tragically her Mum died in an accident while jumping her horse. Kate was only twelve years old. Three years later her Dad returned to his family in Louisiana, taking her with him.

She was glad she kept a partially packed suitcase at her French Quarter apartment. Luckily she found a parking spot right out front. She never wore makeup so she only had to rinse her face in cold water, and brush her teeth, before climbing into bed. Reaching over she set her alarm clock. She decided to get up early and finish packing.

SEVEN

Kate's cell phone rang as she was standing in line to board her flight.

"Katie, dear, our little Sarah is back home." Aunt Jenny sounded very relieved. "She was naughty not letting me know where she had gone. She ran into Jimmy Landry, an old school friend. He gave her tickets to a concert. It was just like you said, Dear. In fact she told me how kind Jimmy was to her. You know how Sarah never goes out in public because she thinks she is not very attractive, well, Jimmy gave her the courage to do just that."

"I am so glad, Aunt Jenny. See I told you...nothing to worry about. I have to go. My flight to London is boarding."

"Katie, if you visit your Granny, do give her our best."

"I will. Take care, Aunt Jenny."

Kate rang off then turned off her cell phone.

Jimmy Landry...she hadn't heard his name since Sarah was in high school. And that was more years ago then she liked to remember. She smiled at the thought. Sarah had a major crush on him during their school years.

Kate fell asleep to the drone of the jet engines. Just what she needed. Sleep.

Kate arrived at Heathrow in the morning the next day. She shouldered her backpack and clicked her wheeled luggage into place. Maneuvering through customs she stepped outside to a dreary day.

She hailed a taxi for the long ride directly to London's Paddington Station. She arranged for an overnight sleeper to Penzance, leaving at ten that night. After stashing her luggage in railway storage she ventured out to the first pub that caught her eye. After a substantial meal of Beef and Kidney Pie and a glass of hearty red wine she walked around looking in various shop windows, never straying far from the train station. She returned in time to retrieve her luggage and board the train, exhausted. She was very grateful for a sleeper.

The next morning she arrived in Penzance and checked into the Oceanview Hotel, walking distance from the station. It had been the same hotel Mike Greenwald had stayed in five years ago.

In the cool quiet of her room she studied everything in the blue file Mike had given her on Diana Dorsey. But why a postcard within an envelope? Could be so no one could read what she wrote? She went through the pictures he had given her. Diana was a lovely young woman in her late twenties...early thirties. Greenwald was just a few years older. From the date the pictures were taken Kate knew it was pre-Omega days. Diana had light brown hair and from the information in the folder Mike had given her she knew the girl had green eyes. Not tall, not short. They looked happy together. Very happy.

Kate was very careful to appear, to the front desk clerk, like a tourist who had left her tour group and struck out on her own for a tour of Penzance. She picked up a street map from the clerk and stepped outside to a cold, rainy day. It was well into the afternoon. Heavy dark clouds made it look even later.

The Blue Iron Pub appeared quiet but when she pushed open the heavily carved wood front door it was chaos inside.

Music blared from a jukebox in the far corner. Rowdy laughter came from a gang of teenage boys hunched over the pool tables in an adjoining room, all pretending to be pool sharks. Peanut shells littered the dirty, wide plank wood floors. Pictures of patrons in silly costumes, with sillier smiles, decorated the walls.

Kate wondered why a classy lady like Diana had been working in a place like this.

Kate waited for an open stool at the crowded bar and took it.

A short stocky man with curly red hair plastered to his head, sweating profusely, walked up from behind the bar where he had been in conversation with some of his cronies. He mopped his face with a dirty kitchen towel he threw back over his shoulder.

"What's a racy filly like ye doing around here?" He leaned in close to her.

"And you are?" Kate didn't flinch. She held her own.

"Billy Flynn. Owner of this fine establishment and ye are?"

"Seeing the sights. Just another tourist." Instinctively she didn't trust him.

"Traveling alone?"

"Not exactly. I'm with friends but they wanted to go one way and I wanted to come here. It's just a brief stop for me." Kate knew it was never a good idea to tell anyone she was alone. She had set up the tourist story at the hotel in case anyone checked up on her.

"What a shame. I thought you were here because of my ad."

"You mean the one that read Good looking man seeking woman to enjoy fun times?"

"You did read my ad! There were two. The other one said I was looking for a buyer for this pub." A huge smile broke across his face. The very idea that this racy filly thought he was a good-looking man made him sweat even more. He was looking to sell the bar, that was true.

"Did you have it appraised?"

"I sure did. This place makes a lot of money. If I sell I could travel the world first class. Want to come?"

"Sounds good to me.

She was flirting big time. And he loved it. But then he remembered that the last woman who noticed him also broke into his vault and took his profits for an entire week. That thought sobered him up immediately. "So what will ye have, darlin'?"

"Something good."Kate bantered back.

She wanted to say a twenty-one year old single malt but figured that wasn't on the drink menu.

"By the way, I didn't catch ye name."

"That's because I didn't give it. I'll have a glass of white wine."

"Oh, a fancy lady, are we?" He swiped the counter in front of her with his grimy towel.

Kate wanted to shrink back. "Yes, actually." She smiled. With her American accent no one would take her for Lady Kate, granddaughter of a Duke. "So, Billy, it looks like you have a full house. Are you by yourself behind that big old bar?"

"Nah. Got a girl working for me but she's not here tonight. She'll be back tomorrow."

"Anywhere you might recommend for a good meal?"

"Ye mean outside of the fine pub food we serve here?" He laughed. "Where are ye staying?"

"The Oceanview Hotel."

"Good food there."

"So many lovely places to see. I'm sorry I don't have more time." Kate laughed gaily and pushed her hair off her shoulder, a sight many men loved to see.

Kate knew the bartender wanted to linger but his attention was taken by a new arrival, a tall man with long black hair tied behind his head. The big guy had a colorful red scarf around his neck and when he swung his head around in her direction she caught a glimpse of a gold hoop earring in his left ear. The tailored suit he was wearing made him look like a Gypsy businessman. She couldn't see his eyes but she bet they were as close to black as possible. He was, for a better word, lurking at the other end of the bar with a scowl on his face that made two or three people move aside and give him a lot of room as he hunched over. He looked like what she imagined a hit man for the Gypsy Mafia would look like.

Billy quickly placed a glass of white wine in front of her. "I'll be back."

"I'm counting on it."

Kate noticed the sign for the loo was just beyond where the big guy was sitting. Taking her glass of wine she slowly made her way down the bar. She caught the end of their conversation. Billy was placating him saying Claire would be back at work tomorrow night. Kate hurried away. She heard enough to realize that Billy had female bartenders and this particular one was of interest to the big guy.

Kate ate a small meal at the hotel.

The next morning she put on jeans, a white shirt, navy v-neck sweater and a navy Brooks Brothers gabardine blazer. Wearing a sensible pair of black leather jogging shoes she was off with a list of places to visit and people to talk to about Diana Dorsey.

By late afternoon her entire day had been difficult. No one knew anything.

Her luck changed when she spoke to Shirley McBride the owner of Rose Cottage the last place Diana had stayed before she disappeared. Shirley had kept a box of Diana's things in case she came back one day.

Shirley seemed relieved to turn over the box to Kate. "I don't have much information to give you. I liked her. She was a sweet girl and paid in cash each week, she did. Her only friend was a girl she worked with, Claire, the niece of the owner of the pub. Two weeks after Diana disappeared I got a letter from New York, it's in the box. Then a woman from America called looking for her money, she said. Apparently Diana had been sending her monthly money orders. The woman had been drinking. She said to tell Diana her Dad was one week dead and buried. Just like that. She said Diana would be happy to know that. I told her Diana was not here. She said she didn't much care as long as she sent her the money. I felt sorry for Diana. I asked her name in case I saw Diana. She said it was Mrs. Send Me The Money and laughed. That's all I can tell you and from what the woman said Dorsey was not Diana's last name."

Looking through the box Kate came across Diana's diary and a large stack of unopened letters from Mike Greenwald.

"Anything to drink, dear?"

"I'd love a glass of water."

When Shirley McBride left the room Kate pulled out the envelope from New York. She could feel the intense hatred from the woman who had written the one page inside. Sparse of details, it read, 'Diana, your lousy drunk father died like the rat he was...drowned in the river. He's buried in a pauper's graveyard. So where's my money? You ain't sent me a money order in a long time. If I don't get one right away I'll make sure everyone knows who you are and where you come from, Miss High and Mighty. What then, huh?'

Kate felt sorry for Diana. The girl had created a new happy life for herself until she ran into the wrong people. The one right thing in her life was Mike Greenwald. She had to bring Diana home.

Mrs. McBride returned with a cold glass of water. They made casual talk for a few minutes. Thanking Mrs. McBride for keeping Diana's things Kate asked if she would hold the box a little longer and mentioned it would be best not to tell anyone she had been asking about Diana. She took the diary and the letters with her.

After she left the cottage she knew her only hope was Diana's friend, Claire, who would be working at the Blue Iron Pub tonight. Mrs. McBride told her that The Blue Iron pub was closed on Monday and Tuesday.

EIGHT

It was four in the afternoon when she stopped at a cafe for tea, sandwiches, and cakes. Having lived with her Granny for so many years she still observed tea at four.

Kate, wanting to look like a tourist, window-shopped until near seven then casually made her way to the tavern carrying a few items purchased and wrapped in colorful paper. In the coolness of the entryway she wondered where the crowd from last night had gone. It was deserted except for a young couple playing pool and three old men at the bar. Kate sat on a stool closest to the front door. A girl, who had been washing glasses behind the bar, dropped her rag and walked over to Kate.

"Never seen ya before. Just passing through?"

Kate didn't see Billy anywhere around but just in case she lowered her voice almost to a whisper. "Are you Claire?"

"I am."

"Maybe you can help me. I'm looking for Diana Dorsey. She used to work here."

The girl looked sad when she heard Diana's name. "She was my friend. She---"

At that moment Billy materialized from a door at the other end of the bar and headed towards the two girls. He had a big smile on his face. Claire looked over her shoulder. When she turned back Kate saw a flash of terror in the girl's eyes.

"I'm staying at the Oceanview Hotel." Kate whispered before Billy arrived.

Claire raised her voice and laughed. "My Uncle Billy here is the owner, he'll take ye order." The girl moved down the bar.

Kate discreetly watched the girl, with her back to the bar patrons, furtively writing something on a small piece of paper. She needed to buy time.

Billy called over his shoulder. "Claire, white wine for the lovely lady."

Kate gave him a sweet smile. "Thank you, Billy, you remembered."

The place was starting to fill with thirsty patrons. Someone called his name from the other end of the bar. He leaned close to her and whispered suggestively, "I hope we can talk later."

"Maybe." She made it sound like a promise. She just knew this guy was trouble.

"Did you give a lot of thought to traveling the world with me?" He smiled.

"Maybe?" She smiled back. How he could make a smile look greasy she didn't know.

Billy rushed off satisfied with the way things were going.

Claire set the wine in front of her. Her eyes went to the bottom of the glass before she quickly moved away.

When no one was watching Kate slid the glass to the edge of the worn wood counter and a small folded note fell into her left hand hidden under the bar. She slipped the note into her pocket. As soon as she finished her glass of wine she retrieved her bag of tourist gifts, made excuses to Billy and paid the bill, leaving a very generous tip.

It was dark outside. Kate walked until she was out of sight of the pub and no one was around. She pulled out the note.

> Nine PM. Go left out of hotel.
> Walk two blocks to 260 Main Street.
> Wait in doorway.
> Do not talk to anyone about Diana.

Walking back to her hotel, Kate thought about Claire. She looked like she was in her late twenties. Kate wondered why she was working in a dive like the Blue Iron Pub. Even if Billy was her Uncle, the girl had a gentle ethereal beauty and Billy Flynn was the kind of man who destroyed innocence.

Getting back to her hotel Kate made a dinner reservation for seven-thirty. Billy Flynn was right about one thing…the food was good.

At close to nine she turned in her key and said she was going for a nightly walk. Following Claire's directions she turned left. The streets were deserted. Two blocks down, approaching the address on Main Street, she heard a sound. Kate stopped and saw Claire standing in the shadows of a doorway.

Claire beckoned to her. She opened a front door to the three story grey stone building and went inside. Kate followed. "I have a flat on the second floor." She whispered.

"Enter and do everything you usually do, okay? And be sure to turn a radio on loud just in case the apartment is wired."

Claire nodded.

Kate wondered what she was getting into but she was grateful for Martial Arts training. She followed Claire up the creaky wood stairs.

Using her key to open the first door to the left at the top of the stairs she whispered, "Wait here," and disappeared into a dark room. An overhead light went on followed by the sound of drapes being drawn. She turned on the radio.

Kate walked in and shut the door behind her. She quickly made a visual tour of the small room. There was a mini kitchen against one wall, a single bed and chest of drawers against another. A door across the room probably led to a bath. There was a picture of Claire and a woman standing in front of the pub. They looked so much alike and had that same quality of refined innocence. They both had long blonde hair, and a slim build.

"Your Mum?" Kate pointed to the picture, keeping her voice low.

"Yes." She handed the picture to Kate who scanned it carefully before handing it back.

"How about starting at the beginning."

"Please, don't tell anyone I talked to you. Especially my uncle."

Claire looked panicked.

"Of course I won't."

"My Dad met my Mum, Mary Claire, in Australia. My Mum's family were fourth generation sheep farmers. My Grandfather published articles about raising sheep, which was something my Dad wanted to do in Penzance, so my Dad wrote to him and my Grandfather invited him to visit the farm. He met my Mum and they fell in love. They married and I was born a year later. We lived in a large log cabin not far from the main house. I was eighteen when my Dad's parents died and he inherited some property. We moved to Penzance, my Dad's home. Going to Cornwall was just supposed to be a short visit. Just to sell the land. My Dad was talked into investing in The Blue Iron Pub with his brother, Billy. The short visit turned into a long time. A year later my Dad died in an accident. Mum inherited his share of the Pub. From that moment on Uncle Billy tried to get my her to marry him but she wouldn't. She wanted to take me back to Australia but she had to sell my Dad's property and a house he owned. My uncle drove away any buyers. Two months ago my Mum disappeared. I know my uncle had something to do with it."

"Why didn't you contact your family back in Australia?"

"I wanted to, but Uncle Billy said my Mum had gone somewhere for him. She would be back soon. My Grandfather was ill and Grandmother was taking care of him. I didn't want to burden them so I didn't say anything about my Mum disappearing. I believed

Uncle Billy when he said that she would be back soon. Then Diana came to work at the pub. We became friends. She was going to help me find my Mum. Diana met an American and they fell in love. The guy left town but Diana confided in me that she planned on joining him. She was going to tell him about my Mum and he would help me. She said the next day she would tell Uncle Billy that she was moving to New York. She disappeared that night after work. I saw my Uncle put a lot of money in a safe in the office. Then a man started hanging around the pub. I'd never seen him before. He was tall, with black hair. I overheard my Uncle talking to him. He called him Roman. Later someone asked who Roman was and my Uncle said he was a big man in the Gypsy Mafia, not someone to cross."

"Do you know what happened to Diana?"

"I overheard Roman telling my Uncle that he would pay him even more next time. The man said the boss liked the last one. I couldn't hear anything else. Their voices were muffled. Later, after Roman left, my Uncle said I had to turn over my part ownership in the pub to him, and the deed to my Mum's house and land, or he would let them take me, too. After my Dad died my Mom gave everything to me. I didn't want to but then he said he would send his men to Australia and hurt my Grandmother. I was so scared I signed all the papers. He gave me this rental flat to live in. Then Roman disappeared for a while until just a few days ago. Earlier this afternoon Roman showed up at the pub and Billy took him into his office upstairs. I listened at the

door. I was careful. My Uncle told Roman it was time for me to go. I
could hear clicks. He was opening the safe. Roman said The Boss was
sending the guys to pick up the money on Tuesday night and they'd
take Claire at the same time. Me! They were talking about taking me!
My Uncle laughed and said they had better send the big Mercedes
with all the money they were taking with them. Roman laughed and
said they always do. Then I heard them leave. There's a back staircase.
When you came in and asked about Diana I was desperate. I took a
chance with the note."

"Did your uncle and the Gypsy guy say anything else?"

"I overheard Roman say the last girl was giving them trouble.
He said that maybe having a friend would help. Then they started
making plans about taking me to some castle in Scotland."

An idea came to Kate. "Listen, you have to get out of town.
My Granny lives not too far from here. I'm going to tell her what's
happening. You can stay at her house. You'll be safe there. I've been
hired to find Diana. I think your Uncle is involved in something bad."

Claire gasped. Tears came to her eyes.

"I've heard they take young girls, alone in the world like you
and Diana, and transport them away from Cornwall, to work in
factories in Ireland and Scotland. They pay them a low wage. The
girls are forced to live in rundown buildings and then they take from
their wages what they call rental expenses and food purchased in the
company store, leaving them with no money. If they complain the

girls are threatened with death. They can't go to the Police because...
sometimes the Police are involved. They work until they die."

Claire's face turned pale. "That's so horrible. I think they are
planning on making me disappear, too?"

"Yes. They were talking about taking you on Tuesday. Do you
work tomorrow? I was told the pub is closed on Monday and Tuesday."

"It is and tomorrow is Monday."

"Perfect. Now tell me...does this building have a back door to a
street or an alley?"

"Yes. From the hallway downstairs there is a back door that
leads outside."

"Is the alley wide enough for a car?"

"Yes."

"Most businesses are closed right now but after breakfast I'll
check out of the hotel, rent a car and pick you up. Watch for me. I'll
drive by the front of the building around eight. When you see me, go
downstairs through the back door to the alley. Don't take anything
with you. No luggage. Nothing. Just your purse. We'll get you a new
wardrobe. I'll be in the alley, behind the building waiting, with the car
idling, get in the backseat and lay on the floor. Cover yourself with a
blanket or coat you'll find there. I don't want anyone to see you until
we are well away from here. Do you understand?"

"Yes...yes." She grabbed Kate's arm. "Thank you!"

"Leave your apartment in the same condition you usually do.

If you normally make your bed then make your bed. Understand? Remember, from now on you act like nothing is out of the ordinary. Do not call anyone. Do not tell anyone you're leaving. Write out a list of to do things like go to the bank, go to the dry cleaners...stuff to do. Leave it on the kitchen table. If someone comes in here looking for you they'll think you're running errands. Got all that?"

"Yes."

"After I leave count to two hundred, slowly, before you turn off the radio. Go to bed at your usual time. Turn off all the lights on your way to bed. We want everything to look normal in case someone is watching you. Okay?"

Kate checked out the door leading to the alley. The back of the building faced the back of another windowless building. Perfect for not being seen. She slipped out the back door and casually strolled back to her hotel stopping at the front desk.

"I'll be checking out in the morning."

"Such a short visit." The night clerk placed her room key on the counter.

Kate smiled. "I'll be back. I was traveling with some friends and I'm going to join them for a few days in Fowey. I think that's the name of the town. Do you have a map of Cornwall?"

"Yes." The night clerk reached under the counter and pulled out a map. He circled Fowey then refolded the map and put it next to her room key.

"Thank you, uh..."

"Mikey."

"Could you arrange a rental car for me for tomorrow, early? Four door compact is fine. Automatic even better."

"Of course. Do you want breakfast before you leave?"

"Oh yes, wouldn't miss it. Breakfast starts at seven, right?"

The clerk nodded.

"I'll leave after that."

"Very good. I'll have the car here early."

"Oh, maybe when I return it might be late. Can I leave the car in front of the Hotel?"

"Yes. Just lock it. Leave the keys under the mat. We'll take care of it. Will you be staying with us on your return?"

"I'm not sure where my friends want to go. I'll call ahead if I am."

Kate's room was on the second floor. She took the stairs. When she was home breakfast was usually a cup of tea and cold buttered toast but right now she had to look like every other tourist...normal... everything normal. She definitely didn't want to look too eager to leave. She gathered her key, the map, and went up the stairs.

Mikey watched her disappear up the stairs before he picked up the phone. "The American girl is leaving tomorrow."

"Where's she going?"

"She said she had been travelling with friends and she's going to Fowey to meet up with them. She ordered a rental for tomorrow. After breakfast she's checking out. She said she'll be back."

"Call me when she goes in for breakfast."

"Done."

"Good job, Mikey. You will be compensated, as usual.

NINE

Bracing a chair under the doorknob Kate fell into an uneasy sleep.

Her small alarm clock went off at six-thirty. Kate was packed and ready to leave right after breakfast. She paid her bill and signed the paperwork for the rental, promising to return the car to the hotel. A dark blue compact was waiting for her in front.

Kate had the key in the lock when she heard a familiar voice.

"Where ye off to so early in the mornin'?"

Kate didn't have to turn around to know it was Billy from the pub. He was standing there sweating like he'd just run five miles. His curly red hair was plastered to his head. His close set brown eyes were watching her very carefully.

"Well, hello there. I'm joining my friends in Fowey, I think that's the place, for a few days. At least I think so. With them I never know where we'll go." Kate waved her map in the air. "Thank goodness for road maps. See you later." Kate got in the rental car. Her heart was racing.

Billy leaned into the car window. "Have ye seen Claire?"

"Claire?"

"The girl working at the pub last night."

"The one behind the bar? No, sorry. Why, where is she?"

"I don't know. Thought I'd check the hotel. Sometimes she picks up a little extra money working in the restaurant during the morning breakfast."

"Thank you for recommending the restaurant here. The food is really good."

"Oh, never mind. I'm sure she'll show up."

"Bye now." In her rear view mirror she could see the Gypsy guy from the bar get out of a small black European car. The guy's so tall. Where does he put his legs? Kate mused. He shut the door and leaned against it. Billy headed into the hotel.

Kate pulled away from the curb hoping Claire was waiting for her. She quickly found Claire's street. The drapes were open. She pulled around into the alley behind the building. Claire came rushing out.

The car came to a stop only long enough for Claire to jump into the back seat and lay on the floor. She covered herself with a raincoat she found there. At the end of the alley Kate accelerated and took a left turn heading for Fowey.

"Are you okay?"

"My phone rang. I didn't answer it. It was my uncle. He left a message saying he was coming over and would wait for me if I wasn't there. He said we were going somewhere. I ran down to the store room next to the back door."

"That tall guy you told me about...Roman...he and your uncle were looking for you at the hotel. I think they were planning on taking you now and holding you until tomorrow night. You got out just in time." Claire started crying very quietly. "You're okay now. Stay covered until I tell you it's safe. I think it would be a good idea to give me your cell. Your uncle can track you with it."

Claire handed over her phone. Kate tossed it into a nearby trashcan. She laughed. "Let him track that!"

Kate followed the map towards Fowey.

TEN

Jimmy Landry drove into New Orleans just in time for the first day of Jazz Fest, a two weekend celebration of Jazz. The number of tourists that came for the music festival every year almost rivaled the crowds that showed up for Mardi Gras. Where Mardi Gras was a day and night of nonstop dancing in the streets while drinking, Jazz Fest was mostly a time for sitting, listening, and drinking. The women at Jazz Fest were young, smart, and not easily misled. To Jimmy that meant a challenge, but one he loved to overcome.

He drove through huge wooden doors that had once accommodated carriages in the 1800s. A flick of a remote and the doors silently slid shut blocking off all noise of the French Quarter. Years ago, when prices were still reasonable, Jimmy had purchased this house. It afforded him the thing he wanted most--total privacy. The carriage entry had a door that led through double doors with a double parlor flanking each side of a hall. A well equipped kitchen and dining room faced a small courtyard. A single bedroom and bath occupied the whole second floor. A perfect bachelor pad. And very convenient for his nightly pursuits when he was in town.

He took a bath and dressed like a vampire tour guide. Girls love it. He preferred to pick a young woman out of the crowd walking the streets of the French Quarter. She would be young, alone and excited about being on her own, maybe for the first time. He loved the ones who were eager to be independent. He would befriend her, a stranger to New Orleans himself, so he told her. He walked not too close, not too far. Just enough to gain her confidence. He would tell her he was going to a party. Would she like to come? They always said yes. They wanted to make a meeting into a romance. So when they went home to their old life they could tell everyone that they had met someone who was handsome and rich, every mother's dream for her daughter, and it seemed promising. He was coming to visit her the following weekend and maybe meet her parents. They said he might be the one. What they got instead was an ending to their dreams, washed in bleach, and folded into the bottom of a chest, with the top drawer holding fishing gear, securely packed into the back of Jimmy Landry's car.

After the first weekend Jazz Fest made the headlines in the Times Picayune. A young girl was missing or maybe misplaced. After all it was New Orleans. Everyone knew that the Crescent City was number one in crime, right up there with great jazz and fabulous restaurants.

Come Monday morning Jimmy packed his leather luggage and headed for his job selling million dollar yachts in Miami. In just a few weeks it would be time for The Hemingway Lookalike Festival followed by Pirates Week, both in Key West. There were no cheap motels like in New Orleans along Airline Highway. Key West was all class. The women who came to have fun had money to spend, a lot of it, and he was only too happy to relieve them of their spare change.

Jimmy easily found not just one this time, but three willing young girls who were looking forward to a sophisticated French Quarter party and a long night ahead on the arm of the handsome, Pierre Duval. After all they were three friends. Together. There was safety in numbers, right? The bare mechanical hum of the wooden carriage doors closing excited him for what was ahead.

Many hours later he drove carefully out of town. It wouldn't do to catch the attention of a state trooper who needed one more to fill his quota.

Years ago with his first big paycheck Jimmy bought a fishing camp right on the bayou. A back staircase led right down to a dock. He didn't worry about neighbors since the fishing camp came with one hundred acres of swamp, snakes, and mean alligators. A pirogue was chained and locked to a concrete post at the end of the dock. Jimmy carefully placed a tarnished metal bucket into the bottom of the boat followed by three large black plastic bags. Pushing off from the dock the pirogue silently drifted through the dark waters. He was eager to see the small pinpoints of light reflecting in the eyes of the gators as they slid off banks and between Cypress trees, letting him know they were awaiting a very tasty meal.

He opened the bags and slid out the body parts. A giant thrashing of snouts and tails let him know everything would be consumed this evening.

He waited and watched as one by one, sated with the feast, they disappeared back into the darkness of the bayou.

Before securing the pirogue once again to the concrete post, he reached down and pulled out the floppy hat. He smiled. Three at once. That was a first for him. He'd take a break for a while. At least until the Key West festivals started up.

ELEVEN

Sometime during the drive Claire woke up. They stopped for a small lunch and Claire moved into the passenger seat.

Kate checked her map then headed towards a small village near the ocean. Arriving in Fowey she drove down a winding private road. A three story manor house came into view. Kate drove around to the back and parked. She opened the doors to a grey stone windowless garage and switched the rental car for a small compact car purchased for the staff when they were in house. The rental car might have a tracking device but Granny's car didn't. No loose ends, Kate thought. It wasn't by chance she had come here. Granny had grown up in this house. Whenever she stayed here she sent servants to take care of the cooking and cleaning. She explained to Claire what was happening. If anyone checked, she was in Fowey just as she had said. She'd swap for the rental car on her way back.

She had another one hour drive to get to Greystone Abbey. Finally she was home. The family crest displayed above the center of the ornate black wrought iron gates. Driving down a winding road, surrounded on both sides by forest, she had an occasional glimpse of parts of an estate with ten turrets and twenty brick chimneys extending from the blue/grey slate roof. Kate thought the magnificent Abbey looked like a castle in a fairytale.

"Where are we?" Claire sat up and looked around in amazement.

"This is where I grew up. After my Mum died we lived here until my Dad took me back to his family in Louisiana. Granny will take good care of you. I have to go back to Penzance tomorrow. You are safe here. But your uncle will not stop trying to find you. He might track you through any phone calls you make to your friends. That's why we tossed your old cell. Forget your past life until this is over. Don't contact anyone. Not anyone. Not even with my Granny's phone. You might put not only yourself but my Granny in danger."

"I understand. How can I thank you for saving my life?"

"Just lay low and out of sight until this is over. And no phone calls."

"Do you think my Mum might still be alive? Do you think she's in the same place with Diana?"

"I hope so. I'll do my best to find her or find out what happened to her."

"Thank you." Claire whispered.

Kate got out of the car and looked around. Claire climbed out right behind her. Nothing had changed, Kate thought. She had lived here for the first twelve years of her life and was used to the beauty of the house well placed on a cliff overlooking the sea with huge boulders and crashing waves.

The massive front doors opened and Kate recognized the three servants who came out. They stood in line. Dawson was Granny's butler, Eric, the first footman and Sara was granny's ladies maid.

"Dawson!" Kate was happy to see the gray haired butler who moved slower than he did years ago.

"Lady Kate! Welcome home."

"Thank you!" Kate laughed.

"Her Ladyship has missed you." Tears filled his eyes.

"Lady Kate?" Claire whispered behind her hand.

"It's complicated." She whispered back then raised her voice. "This is Dawson, my Granny's butler. Eric is the first footman and Sara is my Granny's ladies maid."

"Her Ladyship will be home shortly. Sara will assist you and your guest."

"My bags are in the trunk. But my friend is traveling light."

The girls watched the footman retrieve Kate's bag, backpack and carry them inside.

Kate spoke quietly to the butler. "Dawson, it's really important no one knows I'm here and especially that my friend is staying here."

"Ahh...you're under cover."

"So to speak."

"We will not say a word."

"I knew I could count on you." Kate joined Claire as they entered the massive front doors. Kate was struck at once by the coolness and quiet of the entry. "What happened to the staff? There were at least fifteen in residence when I left."

"After his Lordship died, her Ladyship decided she had no need of a large staff. Most were older than me. Her Ladyship provided very generous pensions for everyone who worked here. Very generous indeed. Now it's just Eric, Jones, the cook, and Sara besides being a lady's maid she helps cook in the kitchen. There's O'Malley, the housekeeper, and Thomas, our gamekeeper and driver, who will be arriving shortly with Her Ladyship. And Thomas' son, Eddie, is our stable hand. Would you like to go to your room first?"

"No. I'd rather be downstairs when she arrives. My friend will be staying in the Blue Room."

Eric took Lady Kate's luggage upstairs. Sara started a fire in the spacious Drawing Room off the entryway, making the room cozy. Tea, sandwiches, and little cakes were brought in on silver trays. Crystal chandeliers were lit.

"The flowers you sent to her Ladyship for the Fourth of July were lovely. She was very happy." A small smile broke Dawson's usual serious demeanor. "I do not think we have that holiday over here. Is that an American custom?"

"Definitely."

He smiled. "Her Ladyship will be home shortly."

"Dawson, I need to make a personal call. Please let me know when her Ladyship arrives."

He nodded and stood at the door.

She turned to Claire. "I'll be right back. The tea cakes are wonderful. Try the tiny cucumber sandwiches. I love them."

Kate left the Drawing Room and walked down the hall to the library, her favorite place. Not wanting to leave a cell phone trail she used the house phone. She called one of the numbers Mike Greenwald had given her.

A message machine picked up the call.

"Mr. Greenwald, this is Kate Bodine. I found out that Diana Dorsey was leaving her job at the Blue Iron Pub to join you in New York. Then overnight she disappeared. I have her diary and some letters I'm sending to you. I believe Diana is alive. Information leads me to an isolated rural area in Scotland. I believe that Billy Flynn, the owner of the Blue Iron Pub, is involved in her disappearance. I will be in touch."

Taking a piece of stationery from her Granny's desk she copied Mike's address and left it in the diary.

Just as she finished Dawson held the door open.

"I left a diary and some letters on the table. Inside the diary you'll find an address for Mike Greenwald. Please mail all of it to him as soon as possible."

"You can rely on me."

"I have a few more calls to make. Please tell my guest I'll be a bit delayed. I'll join her when I'm finished."

"I will." Dawson nodded and left the room.

Shutting the door Dawson almost collided with Sara.

"Mr. Dawson" Sara was out of breath, "Her Ladyship is arriving."

"M'Lady will be pleased."

Dawson and Sarah stood at attention outside.

Seconds later a long black touring Rolls Royce pulled up. Thomas, her Ladyships' driver, rushed around to open the car door.

An elegant woman emerged from the backseat. She walked briskly which was amazing for an eighty year old woman. She carried a silver topped cane but only occasionally did she use it for the job it was intended for.

"Your Ladyship, Lady Kate is here." Dawson was happy to announce the news.

"What a wonderful surprise!"

"She's making a phone call in the library." Dawson held the front door open while Thomas gathered boxes in various pastel colors from the boot.

"Let me know when she's ended her call."

"She brought someone with her."

"Yes?" Her dark grey eyes lit up. One could see the resemblance to her granddaughter. Only her once blonde hair was now silver.

"Her friend is in the Drawing Room." The moment Lady Cathryn saw the young girl she felt she knew her. Standing at the fireplace was a tall, willowy young girl, with soft blonde curls falling around her shoulders and down her back. Dark green eyes expressively looked at her.

Lady Cathryn took her hand. "Please sit with me. You look like someone I knew. Someone from long ago."

Claire smiled. "My name is Claire Flynn."

"Where are you from, Dear?"

"Australia, but recently living in Penzance. I was looking at your rug. It's an Aubusson. My Granny has an identical one in our library at home."

"Really."

"She had two but she gave one as a wedding gift to someone she was best friends with at a boarding school in Switzerland."

Lady Cathryn smiled. No wonder the girl looked so familiar. She looked so much like Wally, a dear friend she lost touch with over the years. "Your Granny's first name, is it Wally?"

"Yes! It's Walden but my grandfather calls her Wally."

"Oh, my dear, your Granny is my very good friend."

"Are you the C.C. like in C.C. and Wally?

"Yes! And you look very much like your Granny."

Claire smiled and took her hand. "She told me all the stories about her good friend, C.C. She said you were the best of friends!"

"This is amazing. Wally's granddaughter here! We must call her immediately."

"We have to wait before we call her. Kate will tell you why."

Dawson, hearing silence from the library tapped lightly on the door and entered. "Her Ladyship has arrived."

Kate gathered her things and rushed out of the room. Granny was sitting beside Claire on the sofa deep in conversation.

"Granny!" Kate, in her joy, ran across the room to give her a big hug.

"I have missed you, Katie." Lady Cathryn smiled and took her hands. "I have a wonderful surprise. Did you know that Claire's Granny is my dear old school friend, Wally?"

Kate's eyes widened. "I can't believe it! And I brought her to you."

"Yes, what a wonderful surprise!" She indicated Kate sit in a dark blue brocade wing chair to her left.

Kate sat down. She smiled at Claire who was beaming. "Claire, do you know how often I heard about Granny's dear school friend, Wally?"

"As many times as I heard about C.C!" Claire laughed.

Granny looked happier than Kate had seen her since her grandfather died. "I wanted Wally to be in my wedding but her mother was ill at the time and she couldn't leave Australia. After that we lost touch. I was busy with my new life, new obligations."

Dawson took that moment to knock and then enter the room. "M'Lady, dinner is served." He announced in a serious voice.

Kate followed behind Granny and Claire who were deep in

conversation.

Not having eaten much that day Claire and Kate did cook's elegantly served dinner proud, then they retired to the Drawing Room for coffee. She fell asleep in a chair beside the roaring fireplace, Kate sat on a small settee. "If it's okay, I would like to leave Claire here for a while. Some very bad people are trying to find her so she has to be protected at all times."

"When I first arrived you were engaged making phone calls. Claire told me everything. And for Wally's granddaughter...anything. Will you be okay, Kate?"

"I have just a little matter to clear up, Granny. Please don't worry about me."

"Of course I worry. I'm glad we have this time to talk. But I don't understand why you haven't touched your inheritance."

"I'm saving it for my old age."

"Why do you do something so dangerous? You don't need to work."

"Oh, Granny. I want my life to mean something. I want to do something that makes a difference. Last year I rescued a seven-year-old girl who had been kidnapped. I have to find someone who's missing right now."

"You have a good heart. I hope when you're finished with what you're doing you'll spend some time here with me."

"I will, Granny."

"I will tell Dawson to alert the staff to be aware of strangers asking questions."

"That's a wonderful idea." Kate smiled. "I think you have the makings of a good detective."

"Oh, no! Not me, dear. I've been remiss in asking you...how is your father? I miss him. Last Christmas he send me a card telling us about Peter. I was very sorry to hear that."

Tears came to her eyes. "Peter was my partner. We were to announce our engagement that weekend. After he died I quit the Police Department."

The elderly butler entered the room after being summoned.

"Dawson, Please tell the staff that our guest is from London. She's staying with us for a long vacation while her parents are abroad."

"I will take care of that immediately." He quietly left the room.

"Kate dear, pay a visit to Red. He misses you terribly."

Kate smiled. "What? Is Red a talking horse now?"

When she was very young her Mum had given her the big red roan so they could ride together. Red was quite old. Kate was overjoyed to know Red was spending his days grazing in a lush green pasture.

"Yes, he speaks on special occasions."Granny laughed. "Now don't be sassy." She took Kate's hand. "I can't believe it. Wally's granddaughter! I must retire. I'm exhausted. I do hope you don't mind. Sara raided your closet for a few things for Claire to wear."

"Of course I don't mind."

"At least until we can get into London to do some shopping."
She laughed and cast a loving look at her granddaughter. "You do
know Harry will be arriving tomorrow."

Kate looked down. She was sorry she wouldn't have time
to spend with her cousin. Upon the death of her Grandfather, and
according to English inheritance laws, Harry became the eighth Duke
of Devon.

Granny, sensed her granddaughter's sadness, turned before
leaving the room. "He always asks me when you're coming home."

"Remind Harry we have a Scrabble game to finish."

"Can you stay at least a few days?"

"I can't. I have to leave tomorrow." She gave Granny a warm hug
and whispered. "I love you, Granny. I will come back. I promise."

Dawson appeared at the door and Granny slowly left the room.

Kate gently touched the Claire's shoulder.

"Did I sleep for very long?"

Kate smiled. "Not long. Granny has alerted the staff to be on
the lookout for strangers. You're protected here."

"Where's Granny?" Claire looked around.

Kate smiled. "Granny?"

"She said I should call her Granny until I'm back with
Grandmother Wally." Tears came to her eyes. "Did she go to bed."

"Yes. Someplace I need to go before I leave tomorrow."

They ascended the wide mahogany staircase. Kate stopped in

front of Claire's door. "Sara is your ladies maid. Check your armoire. There are some clothes you may need until you and Granny get a chance to do some shopping."

"Thank you so much, Kate. You saved my life. I can't wait to tell Grandmother Wally!"

"But not now, Claire. Remember don't call anyone. And one other thing. Never go out of the house without being accompanied by someone. Even having two or more people with you would be better. Will you remember that?"

"I won't forget. I will do what you say. I wanted so much to call my Grandmother but I will do what you tell me. I've heard about CC and Wally all my life. I wanted to call and tell her but it will hold."

"When this is over you will be able to tell her how CC watched over you."

Claire was a gentle soul. How had she managed to survive everything that had happened to her?

"There are a few things I need to show you about the room."

"Sure." Claire was delighted with the room when she walked in. Turning to Kate she clapped her hands. "How wonderful! The walls are a shade of blue that reminds me of the dark blue sky in Australia. Now I know why it's called the Blue Room."

"My room is right next door." Kate smiled at Claire's description. She had chosen the colors in both rooms only the one Claire was in was a darker blue like the color of the sky right before a storm. Her room was baby blue. The silk damask upholstery matched the color of the walls.

"Watch this!" Kate walked over to the fireplace. She pressed the corner of a brick inside the fireplace and a door silently slid open in the paneling. "When I was a young girl I discovered this passageway. It was great fun hiding behind the wall. If you ever have a need to disappear this is one of the secret passages at Greystone." She showed Claire how to open and shut the almost invisible door. There was a switch, to open the door and return to the bedroom.

Claire was delighted with the secret passage.

Kate sat in one of two huge wing chairs flanking the massive carved dark wood fireplace. A fire had been laid and was blazing with warmth.

"Claire, I'd like to ask you a few questions. Do you have a picture of your Mum? I know I saw one in your apartment but I need to see one again. I can't say if I will find her but there is a chance. What is your Mum's name?"

"Mary Claire." Claire searched inside her purse and handed Kate a picture.

"What is something only the two of you shared?"

"Mom always encouraged me to travel and see the world. We were going to go to America. She would say, 'We'll take a road less travelled.'

Kate smiled. "Frost."

"My mother loved reading poetry. Frost was one of her favorites. Kate, there were other girls over the years that went missing. I heard Billy talking about it to Roman one day. He said he only took foreigners who were alone because he had their passports and knew where they lived and threatened to kill their families if they didn't cooperate."

"Do you have names? Did you know who they were?"

"No. They were there before we came. I think my Dad found out what was going on and made plans to get us out of there when he was killed. Then my Mom disappeared. "

"Claire, I'm so sorry."

"Be careful. Billy looks like an idiot but he's very clever."

"You told me there was someone coming on Tuesday night to collect some money at the Pub. That's tomorrow night. They were supposed to take you at the same time. I'll follow them. I hope they'll lead me to the Big Boss."

"The guys who pick up the money from the bar twice a month are the only ones who stay on the second floor of the pub. The money guys drive a big black four door Mercedes."

"Tell me about them."

"The tall one, Bobby, is the big boss' son. He walks with a limp. He gets in fights and last year his right leg didn't heal well. He usually has someone with him. They pick up the profits from the bar. Billy keeps the money in his safe. He keeps his office and his safe locked.

Bobby is the only one who has a key to his office."

"You said you overheard your Uncle say they'd be there to take you."

"Yes."

"Does your uncle follow a schedule or does he show up at the pub anytime he wants?"

"He closes the pub on Monday and Tuesday. I've never known him to show up on those days. He says those are his two days of rest. The guys who come for the money are the only ones who are allowed in the pub when he's not there."

"Got it."

She saw the panicked look on Claire's face. "Don't worry. I'll be very careful. I'm looking for information about missing women like your Mum and Diana."

"Papers are usually in his desk drawers. He has one drawer he keeps locked. I think Bobby has something to do with Diana's disappearance."

"What do you mean?"

"He was there that night. It was a Tuesday. The pub was closed. Diana and I had been called in to do some extra cleaning. I was closing up when Diana left with them. I heard the big one slam the trunk shut and shout something. I didn't see Diana walking home like she usually did after work. That's how we got to know each other. I'd stop and give her a ride and we would talk. We had made plans to get together soon.

The next day Diana had disappeared."

"Okay. I'll see you in the morning." Kate needed time to think. It didn't take her very long to fall asleep to the sound of the crackling logs in the massive fireplace across from her four poster bed.

TWELVE

At breakfast the next morning Dawson opened the door to the dining room and announced, "His Lordship has arrived." He stepped back and Harry walked through the door. His face lit up when he saw Kate. But his smile was nothing compared to the way his eyes lit up when he saw Claire. Kate had never seen what she called instantly falling in love until she saw the look on Harry's face. He finally acknowledged his cousin with a grin, "Hello, Kate."

"Harry, this is our houseguest, Claire."

"Granny called me last night." He took Claire's hand in a most gentlemanly way. "Welcome, Claire. Do you ride?"

Well, you waste no time. Kate thought.

Claire smiled shyly. "Yes, I do. I grew up on my grandparents sheep farm in Australia."

"Wonderful. Granny told me Kate is leaving today. Now I have a new riding partner. Fancy a ride after breakfast?"

Claire looked at Kate.

saddle Red for you, Lady Kate?"

"I brought a friend to stay for a while. She will be riding Red in my absence."

"Red will certainly enjoy that."

Kate smiled. "So we have another person who talks to horses."

"Eddie, saddle Red and Ronan."

"Yes, your Lordship, right away." Eddie raced off to the saddle room to get all the needed supplies. While he led the two horses out and tended to them Kate and Harry looked over the two magnificent riding horses left in their stales. In a short time Eddie would be freeing them to run through twenty acres of fenced pasture, something he did every morning. They returned to the stables on their own in the late afternoon.

"Fancy a ride with us this morning?" Harry patted the soft skin near Roman's nose.

"I wish I could but not now. After I finish this job I plan on returning to spend time with Granny. I hope you'll still be here and we can go riding as we used to."

The sound of boot heels clicking on the cobblestones caused Harry to turn and watch Claire approach them. He smiled. Kate took that as a very good sign.

"I have some things to do before I leave. Maybe I'll see you at lunch. You'll love riding Red. He's a sturdy riding horse."

"Thank you." Claire breathed out elegance. "And Kate, you

have wonderful taste."

Kate smiled. Claire did beautiful justice to her clothes.

Harry gave Claire his full attention as Eddie led out their two horses, Red and Ronan.

Kate walked down the path through the woods to a small lake. The Sanford family mausoleum was a marble building on an island in the middle of the lake. It was built up on a hill with a view of Greystone Manor. It didn't take Kate long to paddle to the island. She remembered the day she crossed the lake, walking with the family up the hill taking her Mum and then, years later, her Grandfather, to their final resting places. Their coffins, inside the building, were next to each other. There were marble benches, inside and out, where the family could sit. She first talked to her Grandfather, then she talked to her Mum for a long time. It was very peaceful. The only sounds were the occasional bird that had entered one of the open windows and built a nest in the ceiling rafters.

Butterflies flew in on delicate wings and out again. This was the closest she could get to her Mum. A breeze gently tossed her hair, the feeling of her Mum's hand was on her shoulder.

After a wonderful lunch Kate knew it was time to get back to Penzance.

Dawson, having been summoned by Granny, appeared at the door to the Dining Room.

She could tell he was worried about her even as smiled broadly and wished her a speedy return. "Safe journey, Lady Kate."

"Thank you." Kate turned to her Granny. "I will wrap this up and be back in no time. I will say goodbye right here. Don't ever forget I love you."

Claire and Harry walked into the Dining Room at that moment. "Granny, I'm sorry we're late. Kate, are you off so soon?"

"I am but I will see you soon." Kate gave Claire a hug. She could tell the fragile girl was trembling. Only she knew how serious Kate's mission had become. "Take care." Claire whispered.

"You take care of Granny for me." Kate whispered back.

"I promise I will."

Dawson, still standing at the Dining Room, held the door open for her. Kate smiled as she followed him to the front door of the Abbey. Eric stored her luggage in the boot and they waved Kate off.

Kate drove directly to her Granny's house in Fowey. The first thing she did was to check to make sure the thread was still in the door frame. The windowless stone building had only one way in through a heavy metal door that was locked. If anyone had gotten in the almost invisible thread in the door frame would have fallen to the ground. Kate was happy to see it was still in place. She quickly switched back to the rental car, leaving her Granny's car in the locked building. So far so good, as she loved to say when all was going as planned.

Kate drove to a village, outside of Fowey, where she filled the rental with petrol and stopped at a teashop for a plate of small sandwiches before heading back to Penzance. She tossed the cash receipts into the back seat, leaving a paper trail in case Billy checked. And she was sure the car was going to be checked. It made sense she was outside of Fowey getting petrol before returning the car to the hotel. No loose ends, Kate thought. They get you every time. She didn't make that mistake.

It was still early evening. Kate drove right to the Pub. If she checked in to the hotel she was sure someone would alert Billy she was back.

Expecting the pub to be closed she was surprised to see the lights blazing downstairs. There was a big black touring Mercedes sedan parked in front along with Roman's car. Kate turned off her car lights and waited about two hundred feet away. Claire was right about the guys picking up the money tonight.

While she was deciding what to do the lights went out upstairs, downstairs and three men came out the front door. Roman got in his car and left. Two men stood in front of the Mercedes arguing about something. The bigger one, who must be Bobby, the Boss' son, was limping. The shorter one was carrying a leather bag. They got in the Mercedes and took off. Kate followed a distance behind, enough not to lose them, but far enough not to be obvious she was there.

Kate had a feeling they would take her to the big boss and his kidnapping operation. It was a lead. If it didn't pan out she would come back and find a way into Billy's office.

THIRTEEN

Jimmy loved his cabin in the bayou. It was on stilts as so many fishing cabins were. He did some fishing and crabbing off his dock and caught up on his reading. He especially liked mysteries. He hated to leave but detoured by way of Mississippi on his way to Miami. Stopping at Joe's Snacks he caught the front page of The Times Picayune, a New Orleans newspaper, out of the corner of his eye. Three local girls from Metairie were missing. The headline said the girls had disappeared on the last night of Jazz Fest. Jimmy managed to keep his cool while he paid for the bag of chips and a six-pack of root beer. He was furious. They told him they were from Kansas in town for music festival.

He never fooled with locals when he was in the Quarter. Too much could go wrong. And he was very careful. Before he left his bayou cabin he had cleaned the trunk of the nondescript Chevy that he used when he was in the Quarter. The Chevy was one like most tourists rented when they came to New Orleans. For his trip back to Miami he swapped the Chevy for an old Ford, with Arizona plates, that he kept

in the closed garage below the cabin. When he was in Miami he drove

a 1967 Mercedes convertible, with Florida plates and used the name

Conrad Benson. If the State Police were looking for a Chevy, that had

been reported for suspicious activity in the Quarter, then they weren't

looking for an old Ford on the way out of town. He made sure there

were no loose ends.

Ready to go, he started driving to his home in Miami. As

was his habit he stopped at Chuck's Diner outside of Tampa. He

loved the burger, fries and malts made the old way. The place was not

very big but put out the best comfort food in the south. Ten swivel

red vinyl stools were secured down in front of a counter. Six red

vinyl booths with an old time miniature Jukebox on each table also

held small toasters, plastic bottles of condiments and stainless steel

napkin holders. Jimmy took his usual seat at the end of the counter

where it was not very loud and he could talk to the owner/chef Chuck

Marciano.

"Hey, Jimmy! The usual, right?" Chuck liked the kid. Chuck

was sixty years old so anyone under the age of forty was a kid to him.

"You know me, Chuck. Predictable."

Chuck disappeared behind the stainless steel counter separating

the cooking grill from the counter where the customers sat. Jimmy heard

the sizzle of the grill, the bubbling sound of the French fries, and the whir

of the blender making the thick malts he was so well known for. Chuck returned in fast time with a burger, fries, and a chocolate malt.

"Dressed just like you like it." Chuck set the platter down in front of Jimmy."

In the South the word dressed meant mayo, lettuce, tomatoes and pickles. Chuck knew Jimmy didn't like pickles so he didn't pile them up on the burger like he usually did for other customers. He put them on the side. Remembering things like that kept Chuck's customers loyal to him.

"I haven't seen you in a while. You've been busy, huh?"

Jimmy smiled. He ate quickly. If only Chuck knew just what he had been doing. "Yeah. Working. You know how it is. I have to pay for that big gas guzzler outside." He laughed. What a joke. People saw him driving that car and figured he was broke. Not the kind of guy who lived in a mansion on the water in Miami and drove a classic Mercedes. "I made a few bucks on a sale in Atlanta."

Chuck laughed. "I bet you're the top salesman in your company. Didn't you tell me you worked for IBM?"

"Nah. I'm a freelancer. You want a computer like a Lenovo. You want an Apple. I can get it for you."

"Wow. Sounds like a good job, Jimmy. Hey, want to hear a joke?

"Sure."

"What does IBM stand for?"

"I think you're going to tell me." Jimmy smiled. He had heard that joke about a million times. He quickly finished his meal.

"I've been moved. IBM. Get it?" Chuck roared with laughter. He loved telling jokes.

"That's a good one." Jimmy grinned and threw a twenty on the counter for his meal. He always paid in cash. Always. "See you next time I'm in town. I want to get to D.C. before dark." He turned at the door. "Where's Kitty? She's not here?"

"She had to take time off. Her daughter, Liddy, is sick. She'll be back next week. I'll tell her you asked about her."

Jimmy pulled out a one hundred dollar bill from his wallet. "This is for her kid. Tell her, okay?"

"I sure will, Jimmy. Thank you!" Chuck wiped his hands on his apron around his waist and pushed the bill under the register. What a great guy! Chuck thought.
He was kind, considerate and good looking enough to make all the girls turn around and look at him when he stopped at the diner for a burger.

Chuck watched Jimmy drive off. One day he's gonna meet the right one and make some lady really happy!

FOURTEEN

Jock had one of those father's instincts. He just wanted to hear Kate's voice and know she was okay. He called Kate's sat phone but it was on answer only mode. Kate had left a message saying she was out of the country. He disconnected the call. That usually meant she had gone to see her Granny in England. It had been too long since he'd talked to Lady Cathryn. He knew even if she wasn't there Kate wouldn't go to England without calling her Granny. He checked the number and dialed.

The butler, Dawson, answered the phone after one ring. Her Ladyship was taking her mid afternoon nap and hated to be disturbed with non essential phone calls but she asked if Mr. Bodine called she wanted to speak to him.

Dawson knocked on the Library door and went in carrying the phone. "Sorry to disturb you, M'Lady, but it's Mr. Bodine on the line.

She took the phone with smile on her face. She liked Jock Bodine from the moment her daughter brought him home to meet her father for his blessing on their marriage. Jock was very charming and his manners were impeccable.

"Jock, my dear, how are you. It's been entirely too long. When are you coming for a visit?"

"Soon, I hope. Is Kate there? Have you seen or talked to her?"

"I have. I was going to call you if you hadn't called me. I'm terribly worried about her. She stayed here last night. She left a few hours ago."

"Did she say where she was going?"

"I understood she was returning to Penzance. She brought Claire with her yesterday and left the dear girl here. Claire told me everything. Kate has a client who engaged her services to find his fiancée. Her name is Diana and she was working for The Blue Iron Pub in Penzance when she disappeared. Claire's Uncle, Billy Flynn, owns the pub. Claire's mother also went missing from the same pub. Claire said she overheard her Uncle say he was going to have her kidnapped and taken to Castle McLaren, someplace in Scotland. Apparently it was the same place her Mum and Diana are being held. Two men, in a black Mercedes, are picking up money from that pub in Penzance tonight so Kate was going to follow them. She said a Gypsy named Roman was also part of this kidnapping gang."

"Do you want me to provide protection for you?"

"Harry is here and he's already arranged security guards 'round the clock."

"I'll call my contacts in Scotland Yard. Don't worry. I'll bring Kate home."

"What do you know about Billy Flynn, owner of The Blue Iron Pub in Penzance and a Gypsy named Roman, and Castle McLaren in Scotland?"

"Plently. If Kate is headed for Castle McLaren in Scotland she's right in the middle of the largest cocaine bust Great Britain has ever seen. Lord James, owner of Castle McLaren, runs the show. He's been producing and trafficking cocaine for years. Interpol has an undercover operative there posing as his bodyguard, Charlie Campbell." Jock came out of The Rib Room where he had earlier joined a table of his fellow officers for lunch. "We have a team in Penzance right now. We picked up a broadcast that Lord James had to speed up a huge delivery to the UK and parts of Europe. His cover is that he builds fast boats for the drug deliveries."

Lady Cathryn twisted the phone cord. "Kate is following two money guys out of Penzance tonight. They will be at The Blue Iron Pub traveling in a black Mercedes. I think they are headed for Scotland and Castle McLaren!"

"Please don't worry. I'll be on the first flight out." Jock worked for the New Orleans Police Department but he was also brought in to work with Interpol, MI5 and Scotland Yard. His skills with Behavioral Analysis Units was ledendary.

FIFTEEN

For a while Bobby followed the Cornish coast towards Scotland.
Then he turned inland. Colin snored in the passenger seat while Bobby
drove, sometimes erratically, waking Colin up off and on. What they
all needed was some strong coffee, Bobby thought. Finally Bobby
yelled at Colin to wake up. They were going to stop and get some coffee
at The Golden Crown. Colin was relieved. He wasn›t sleeping. Who
could sleep with that idiot driving?   Bobby abruptly pulled off the road
and into the parking lot. There were four motorcycles parked near the
front door.

"Bobby, you›ve been here before?" Colin asked getting out of the
car.

"All the time. It›s my stop over. The owner, Milly Murphy, is a
good friend of mine"

"And the bikers? Good friends, too?"

"I've never seen bikers here before but I›m sure she keeps them in
line."

Bobby and Colin debated what to do about the cash bag. Colin
wanted to take it inside, remembering what Bobby›s dad had said about
the money being his responsibility. Bobby wanted to leave it in the car

afraid it would attract attention if he brought it inside the bar. In the end Bobby took a pair of handcuffs from the glove compartment and cuffed the handle to his left wrist.

When they walked through the door the bikers turned to look at them. The first thing they saw was the object cuffed to Bobby›s wrist. They measured just what was so important about that bag. In any case they intended to find out.

"That doesn›t look like someone named Milly." Colin nodded to the biker bartender behind the bar.

"I've never seen him before."

"Get the coffee and let›s go."

Kate waited in the parking lot near the door. A huge commotion came from inside the pub. A bar stool flew out the window followed by screams of terror. She had followed them this far. She wasn›t going to leave now. Not until they got to where they were going. Kate said a quick prayer and walked in like a cool breeze.

Two of the bikers, knives in hand, had Bobby and Colin against the bar. The other two were sitting it out in a drunken stupor.

Bobby and Colin looked like deer caught in headlights with their backs against the bar.

Oh great! Kate thought.

Everybody in the bar looked at her. They figured she was just some lost bitch on her way to a tourist area. Wrong place, wrong time for her.

Think fast! "How ya doin› y›all? Hi, y'all!" She did that little four finger wave which fascinated the bikers. Kate›s accent was more like Alabama than New Orleans but nobody in this room would know that. All the while she was making her way over to Bobby and Colin, whose head was nodding sideways towards his friend›s shoulder, about to pass out. They were bloody with Colin having taken the worse of it so far. She dropped a breath to her lower abdomen to keep from shaking and kept moving.

Sticking her thumb in the direction of the Jukebox over in the corner she gushed, "Hey y'all, does that music box over yonder play When The Saints Come Marching In? I just love that song, y›all, my being a Yank and all!"

She kept one thought in mind...what would her Sensei do?

The bikers were fascinated with this strange talking bitch. Kate felt like a snake charmer who had just dropped into a den of King Cobras.

Just as she grabbed Bobby and Colin and started to drag them out of there, all hell broke loose.

The biker with the leather Marlon Brando cap pushed her aside. He had just raised his ten-inch knife, intent on taking the bag away from Bobby or taking Bobby away from the bag. The bald biker behind him pointed to Kate, warning her to stay away from them. The other bikers, one with a black leather vest and the other with a greasy T-shirt were too inebriated to get involved but yelled to their mates with cheers like "Break ‹im up, good," and "Leave the pieces for the hospital wagon!"

The bartender, despite his attempt to fit in with his leather jacket and scraggly beard, sneaked along the back wall and out the back door.

Kate could not reach the man with the Brando cap and the knife without first going through the bald biker. She took Baldy by the crook of his right elbow and spun him towards her with a loud «Hey!» She hoped her sound and subsequent actions would change Knifeman's intent.

Baldy spun around to find a blonde woman six inches shorter than he as many inches from his nose. He smiled a crooked smile, looking directly into her eyes. That meant he could not see the shin kick she delivered with the inside of her right foot. Her friends on the New Orleans Saints football team would have been proud of her since it displaced Baldy›s lower leg to his rear, tilting his face towards hers. She shifted to her left, replacing her face with a right horizontal elbow, instantly making his smile even more crooked.

Knifeman couldn›t make out what Baldy cried on his way to the floor because the biker›s hands were clamped over his mouth.

Looking Knifeman straight in the eyes just long enough to freeze him, she lifted her right knee to deliver a low side-thrust kick to the back of Baldy›s head. His face slapped against the stone floor and a tooth escaped through his fingers.

Knifeman saw a small puddle of blood around his mate›s face

before he turned back toward the woman. He managed to yell out, "You fu---" before he realized she was no longer where she had been. Another low side thrust to his calf from behind collapsed his right knee. Kate looped her slim right forearm around his neck and began to squeeze in a naked strangle from her Judo days.

Realizing she was not strong enough to make him succumb quickly, she snapped her forearm sideways across his chin, making his neck crack. His left hand immediately went to the back of his neck as he called her «You damn whore,» and stumbled to a vertical position, limping, with his head cocked at an unusual angle.

Kate waved Bobby and Colin back against the bar, an unnecessary action since they were either debilitated, frozen with fear, or both, and were not about to get in her way or help her out. Kate quickly gave a sharp exhale and took a step toward Knifeman who had secured his grip on his knife and was slashing left and right, almost blindly, stumbling forward in hopes of cutting down this irritating bitch.

As he delivered a backhanded slice, Kate arched backward letting a forearm swing past, then entered past his elbow, her left forearm contacting the triceps tendon just above his elbow and her right hand cupping over his wrist. She spun her body clockwise, using his aggressive momentum to power her turning takedown. Knifeman spiraled down to his chest, his chin bumping the stone floor. Still he didn›t release the blade.

Kate leaned into his elbow with her left forearm while placing her right knee under his wrist. She knew that, if he were in better condition, he was big enough to muscle out of this position, but she did not need to hold him long, only long enough to jolt her shoulder toward his elbow, making his hand open and the knife drop to the floor, bouncing once toward the unconscious Baldy.

She delivered one more elbow jolt to cause Knifeman enough pain to occupy him while she rolled to recover the knife. He was stumbling to his feet, his right knee weak, his lower lip bloody, and his left hand bracing his right elbow. He knew that most people would not use a deadly weapon on him. That gave him an edge. Even if he couldn›t have what was in the handcuffed bag, even if those two blokes with the bag ran away, he could have the satisfaction of smashing her pretty face through the jukebox glass, giving her scars she would never forget.

As he lunged at her, she raised her knife hand high as if to slice him from above. His eyes and shoulders went up as she slipped to her knees pulling the knife down to slice his jeans on the left inner thigh. Sliding between his legs, she plunged the knife backward over her left shoulder and into his right butt cheek. He screamed loud enough for the bartender, cringing behind the trash bin in the back lot, to hear him. Knifeman›s right arm was too damaged to pull the knife out and his left hand couldn›t reach around his body far enough to extricate it.

The drunken bikers looked on silently with eyes wide and mouths open. Then they began to laugh. One laughed so hard that he vomited on the other who fell out of his chair.

SIXTEEN

Kate led Bobby, who was half-carrying, half-pushing Colin, out the door, to the car park, and the Mercedes.

"Give me the keys." Kate held out her hand.

Bobby faced her with his arms and legs splayed against the passenger side of the car. "It's my Da›s car." He knew he sounded like a whiny kid but he couldn't help it. If it hadn›t been for this woman they would be picking him up in pieces right now, along with Colin who was passed out right outside the front door.

"I don't care if it›s the Queen›s car. Give me the keys. You are in no condition to drive."

Kate pushed him into the passenger side and climbed behind the wheel. She drove over to where Colin was snoring by the front door and hefted him into the back seat. She stopped at her rental car to grab a valise from the passenger side, put the car keys under the mat and lock the doors. She now had a major headache.

Kate nudged Bobby. "Which direction?"

Bobby grudgingly pointed to the left in a huff. Who was this bossy broad, he wondered? His eyes closed and his head started to tilted toward the soft leather seat.

Using her sat phone she talked as she drove, advising the car company where to pick up the rental. They said they'd be there in the morning.

Bobby opened one eye and stared at Kate. "Where are we going?"

"Good question. I have no idea. I'm not a mind reader."

Bobby burped. He was glad he was still breathing. "Who are you?"

"My name is Kate. It would be a really good time to tell me who you and your friend are and where we're going."

"I'm Bobby and that's Colin. Where did you come from? Are you an Angel of Mercy?" Bobby gave her a somewhat lopsided grin.

"Hardly. I was on my way to finding a Bed and Breakfast and I stopped at that pub to use their bathroom facilities. I was almost hit by a chair flying out a window just as I walked in."

"Lucky for me."

"Sure was."

"I think I'll take a little nap."

"You must be exhausted." Sarcasm was certainly lost on this guy.

"Yeah." He burped again. He leaned his head against the side window and looked at Kate. "I'm going to rest now. It's been a big night."

"Oh, I can see that. Hey, before you pass out, where are we going?"

Bobby gave her a lopsided grin.

"Bobby! I'm talking to you! Where do you live?"

"Castle McLaren." He mumbled.

Before Kate could ask anything else Bobby was snoring.

Colin woke up briefly. "Who are you?"

"I'm Kate and I'm taking you and your friend to Castle McLaren."

"Oh, good. I thought we had died and gone to Heaven."

With that he passed out again.

Not until I find Diana and Claire's mum. Kate thought.

Kate googled Castle McLaren on her smart phone and got the GPS directions. It was on the Irish Sea along the Scottish coast. Current owner for the past twenty-five years was Lord James.

She drove for hours finally leaving the main road to take a path, with a thick forest on either side, big enough for two horse drawn carriages to pass side by side. Finally, after nearly forty miles, Castle McLaren came into view in the distance. After a long driveway it stood majestically against the sky with the ocean thirty feet below.

Kate drove around a massive water fountain with two carved stone horses rearing against each other in the middle. The water in the bottom of the huge bowl splashed up against their muscular flanks. Kate veered to the right around the fountain.

The front door opened and servants came out adjusting their uniforms. Kate figured them to be a butler and a first footman. They were followed by a tall, well built man dressed in black. Probably a bodyguard. He was followed by a man wearing a dressing gown over his pajamas. This must be the big boss. He didn't exactly have a welcome home, son, look on his face. The irritated group walked over to the car.

Kate got out and stood in front of the car.

Bobby staggered out the passenger side. "We made it, Da! Here it is! He unsuccessfully tried to lift the case still handcuffed to his wrist.

"I see. Why don't you introduce me to your friend...the one who was driving my car." He indicated to his bodyguard to get the money bag pronto.

"She saved me life. We stopped at this pub for coffee. Me and Colin were viciously attacked, we were, by a band of robbers. I fought them off and then Kate there stepped in to finish it and extricated us from that horrible place." Bobby exhaled whiskey in a huge burp. Turning to Kate who was doing her best not to smile at Bobby's storyline. "Kate this is me Da and this is Kate...er just Kate."

Meanwhile Colin had climbed into the front seat dragging the girl's valise with him. He was determined to park the car in the six car garage behind the castle. He put down the car window on the driver's side and threw the valise out the window. The headlights were still on so he turned the key and stepped on the accelerator. He waved as he drove past them.

"Just parking the car!" He yelled. Never having driven this car before he didn't expect it to take off like a racehorse out of the gate. In his drunken stupor he screamed as he hit the gas pedal instead of the brake.

Kate wondered if glass was breaking somewhere since his high pitched scream was deafening.

Bobby screamed, in return, since the car was heading straight for him. With lightning speed Kate flew through the air taking Bobby with her, out of the path of the car.

Lord James' bodyguard had backed up the house group.

At the last second Colin violently turned the wheel to the left and ran the huge Mercedes sedan into the fountain, smashing the two stone horses who now lay apart on their backs with their massive legs, and body parts, around them.

Lord James started screaming.

At that moment Kate was trying to push Bobby, who had passed out and was snoring very loudly, off of her.

Concern for the woman who was on the ground underneath his overly large son was the only thing that stopped him from a violent act against the two boys.

Lord James looked ready to blow a fuse. "Carter, would you and Liam get Bobby off that young girl. Charlie, drag that idiot out of my car."

Kate just lay there moaning while Bobby was telling his father in rapid dialogue, once again, about the huge bar fight and how he and Colin had taken down a bunch of bad bloke bikers. "Da, you should have been there. We almost died. Then Kate came in and saved the day with some kind of Haiki Martial Arts stuff." Bobby staggered to his feet while Charlie left to help the still screaming Colin who was trying to crawl out of the passenger side window but was stuck halfway. The driver's side was braced shut by one of the huge body parts of one of the horses.

Charlie pulled Colin out through the window and, unseen, reached under the car for something that he quickly slipped into his pocket.

Kate, who never missed anything noted it was something he didn't want anyone to see.

Lord James turned to Kate who was now standing on only her right foot, deciding that her left ankle was going to be badly sprained. "I'll have my Doctor look at that."

"Honestly, it's only a sprain."

"Then you will accept my hospitality tonight."

"Thank you."

Charlie carried a still screaming Colin and placed him on the ground by Bobby.

Deciding to ignore the boys Lord James introduced Kate. "This is Charlie Campbell, my bodyguard. He's a Yank. He'll look after you." Turning to his bodyguard, "Take care of her ankle."

Charlie took her arm. They slowly made their way towards the massive front doors. "What is Hikia? Must be something new." He whispered.

Kate stopped hopping. "That's Aiki. But you knew that!"

"I did. Just kidding!" Turning to the footman who just stood there. "Liam, her luggage, on the ground. Thanks."

Kate looked him right in the eye. He smiled like he knew just what she was doing here. Now that she got a good look at him. Wow!

A little over six feet tall and well built, with straight dark hair, dark blue eyes and dimples when he smiled. By his accent she guessed he was from New England, probably Boston.

Lord James, carrying the money bag, directed the rescue of the still screaming Colin. Bobby tried to console his friend while his Father stormed past Charlie and Kate into the castle.

Showing great reserve Lord James nodded to a woman waiting by the grand mahogany staircase leading to the upper floors. "Mrs. Callaway will show you to your room. Charlie, I won't need you tomorrow. I put you in charge of our houseguest. And now, I'm going to have a very stiff drink." With that he disappeared into the library, followed by his butler, Carter. "I want those two boys brought to me. Immediately!"

"Yes, M'Lord." Carter put a martini, very cold, very dry, on a table next to his boss and left the room.

Lord James crossed the room and pressed a button inside a bookcase. A silent door opened to a room full of treasures. He dropped the money bag on the floor and sighed. He'd count it tomorrow.

Going back to the library he collapsed into his favorite leather wing chair. Lifting the glass he drank the still cold Martini in one gulp, his favorite way of relaxing.

The door opened and Carter announced the arrival of Bobby and Colin. An overwhelming odor of cheap whiskey preceded them. They stood contrite in front of his chair. Colin had a hard time staying awake.

"Both of you are a disgrace. Colin, when your Da died I said I'd take care of you. If it wasn't for my promise I'd send you to a work house. And Bobby, if you weren't my only son I'd disown you. Right now I'm sending both of you to the dungeon to think about how you can become more responsible. Now get out of my sight."

Carter ushered the two boys out the door. They didn't make a sound. Obviously they knew, by past experience, if they complained then their stay in the Dungeon Hilton would be an extended one.

Carter completed his task and brought the boss another cold, very dry Martini.

SEVENTEEN

Kate hopped up a few steps before Charlie gave a huge sigh, swept her into his arms and continued climbing up the grand staircase.

"Put me down!" She pummeled him with her fists. His chest was so hard it was like hitting iron.

"Tsk, tsk, such language. Not very ladylike, is it?" Charlie couldn't help smiling.

"This is just like Rhett and Scarlett and they didn't end up very well either."

"Really, well I bet Scarlett weighed a lot less than you do and there were fewer stairs."

"I said put me down! Now!" Kate glared at him.

"Can't do that. I have my orders."

Charlie ignored Kate and spoke to the woman waiting nervously at the top of the stairs. "Mrs. Callaway, please run our guest a hot bath, find some pajamas for her, and also a crutch." He talked as he headed for the right wing corridor. He kicked the base of a partially opened door. Walking across the room he unceremoniously dumped Kate into a wing chair, one of two flanking a fireplace.

"Mrs. Callaway will take over from here. I'll be next door, in case you need me. See you in the morning. And, don't go downstairs without me."

"Wouldn't think of it."

Charlie smiled as he walked out the door. He didn't believe that for a second.

Kate felt human after a hot bath, donning silk pajamas and snuggling into a warm bed. Mrs. Callaway was kind enough to bring her a late night sandwich and a glass of warm milk. Before leaving the room the elderly woman lit a fire in the magnificent fireplace.

After finishing her late night snack Kate fell asleep. Her dreams of being swept up in the arms of a handsome man that looked, now that she thought about it, a lot like Charlie who was one of the most irritating men she'd ever met It brought her to a rude awakening, or maybe it was the loud banging on her door.

"What?" She yelled out. What a horrible mood she was in, she thought. Thank goodness she had braced a chair under the doorknob before she went to sleep.

"Open the door."

She checked the travel clock on the slim table by her bed. Was it really nine in the morning?

She recognized Charlie's voice and he didn't sound very happy.

Well, tough, she grinned. "Just a minute."

Climbing out of bed she slipped on the robe that had been provided for her and grabbed the crutch that was leaning against the wall. Clumping over to the door she took her time trying to figure out a plan. She was perfectly capable of walking but it was fast thinking that got her into the castle as a wounded guest so she figured she better keep it up as long as possible. It would give her time to look around and find Diana and she hoped Claire's Mum, too. Before she got to the door she resolved to be very nice to Charlie. Striking up a friendship could be to her advantage.

She moved the chair from under the doorknob and opened the door with a huge smile on her face.

"Hello. Thanks, awfully!"

"For what? And what's with the English accent?"

Kate turned pale. How did she let that slip through? "When in England and all that!" She smiled. "Anyway thanks for helping me last night."

Her smile was dazzling but it didn't fool him. He knew everything about Kate Bodine...Lady Kate Bodine.

"It's my job, remember. Now get dressed!" He sat on a chair outside the door. "And be quick about it."

Kate wanted to slam the door, but thought better of it. She quickly rummaged through her valise and pulled on jeans, a white silk blouse and a dark blue blazer. She pulled her hair into a ponytail and stood there deciding, barrette, no barrette, hair band...hmmm. Hair band, she decided! She finished gathering her long blond hair into a ponytail.

"Put a move on it!" Charlie was getting impatient.

Grabbing her backpack and crutch she hobbled out the door. Standing at the top of the stairs she looked back at him. He grabbed her up and headed down the stairs mumbling something about "High maintenance."

Kate did her best not to laugh. "Where are you from? Let me guess...Boston."

At the bottom of the stairs he put her back on her feet. "Concord, near Boston. Good guess." Pointing to the room off the left of the huge entrance hall. "Breakfast."

"Do you always speak in one word sentences?"

"No." He paused. "Not always."

Kate followed him into a magnificent room. Light blue, her favorite color, silk brocade covered the eighteenth century Chippendale dining chairs. The same silk brocade covered the walls. A large rosewood, marble topped, sideboard stood against the wall laden with silver serving pieces with ornately covered lids.

Two eighteen-light chandeliers, heavy with Waterford crystals, hung at each end of the twenty-foot dining table. A gold twelve candle candelabra centered the table. On one end of the room a blazing wood fire gave warmth to the room.

Kate wondered what Lord James did that was so profitable.

Charlie stoked the fire while Kate piled her plate with wonderful things to eat.

"I talked to Bobby this morning. He told me you saved them from two bad guys armed with big hunting knives. They had the boys with their backs against the bar."

"And your point is?"

At that moment Carter opened the dining room door and Lord James walked in with a very irritated look on his face.

Kate thought it was just what she was feeling, too.

"What are you and Charlie up to?" Lord James gave him a sideways glance. "Something about knives?"

"Bobby told me that Kate saved his life when she disarmed two men with hunting knives at that pub last night."

Lord James tucked into his breakfast with gusto. He gave the girl a glance, "Well done, Kate. Charlie, you might learn something from her."

"I bet I actually could teach you a few things, Charlie." Kate smiled sweetly which aggravated him even more. She knew it would.

"I bet you can't." He moved away from the fireplace.

Kate took a dainty bite of the sausage, eggs, and tomatoes. It was either that or fling it at that irritating man. But, lucky for him, she loved an English breakfast far too much.

Charlie sat next to Lord James but turned away anything to eat.

He preferred a cup of coffee instead.

Lord James smiled. "As I said last night I won't be needing you today. Why don't you get the wheelchair from the servants quarters and show Kate the gardens."

"Thank you, Lord James. I would love to see the Castle gardens. I love flowers. They look lovely from my window. And I'd love to go down the ocean path and see the water." Kate smiled ever so sweetly.

"I bet you can see that from your window, too." Charlie frowned.

Kate gave it right back. One thing she could do with ease was sarcasm. "Oh, yes, I do, and it's so...so peaceful except..."

Lord James looked up from his breakfast. "Yes?"

"I could hear boat engines making ever so much noise last night."

"They have to be checked. I build racing boats for the European market. We were testing them. They leave tomorrow for buyers in Nice and London."

"I see."

"Have you ever driven a power boat?"

"I have. And I sail, too."

"Really! Charlie you'll have to show our guest what we do. We're going to test them again at midnight. Is that too late for you?"

"I always stay up late. Thank you, Lord James."

Charlie turned and gave her a steely look. "Then that's what we'll do."

You'd probably love to throw me off the cliff, too, Kate thought as she gave him her most charming smile.

Charlie pushed his chair back. "Lord James." If you'll excuse me I'll get the wheelchair. I'll be out in the hall when our guest is ready."

Charlie passed Carter entering the dining room. The butler had a sealed note in his hand. He handed it to Lord James.

Kate watched Lord James open the message and quickly scan the contents. She kept her eyes on her plate but didn't miss a thing. He threw his napkin down and pushed away from the table, the note clutched tightly in his hand.

"Kate, my dear, Charlie will be great entertainment for you. Do not expect me for dinner."

"Thank you for your kindness, Lord James." Before she could say anything else he disappeared from the dining room. She heard him say something to Charlie in the grand entrance hall and then he was gone.

"Ready to go?" Charlie stood in the doorway. "Stay where you are. I have a wheelchair for you." Carter held the door to the dining room open while Charlie brought the wheelchair next to where Kate was sitting.

Kate did a great job pretending to struggle to get into the chair.

Charlie thanked Carter as the butler rushed to open doors as fast as Charlie passed through, one to another.

Outside they headed for the very large English garden. Charlie quickly pushed her under a trellis heavy with flowering vines. She could swear he made sure low hanging branches smacked her in the face as they rushed down the garden path. Kate had never paid much attention to flowers so she was at a loss to name anything she saw. Anyway she was careful to keep her mouth shut before she ended up with leaves and bugs stuck in her teeth. The man was insufferable!

When they reached a bed of roses Charlie came to an abrupt stop. A little too abrupt, Kate thought. He pointed to the roses. "We're safe outside. The inside of the castle and the stone house on the water are not safe. We are videoed and recorded everywhere but the bathrooms. By the way, I know who you are."

Kate pointed to a white rose tree. "Really, and who am I?"

"I spoke to Jock before you arrived. He told me he talked to your Granny. Lucky for you Claire had told her everything. Your father had a tracker attached to the Mercedes, which I managed to retrieve, while I was pulling Colin out of the car last night."

"Oh great. You could have told me last night before you manhandled me going up the stairs."

"I don't believe Scarlet called it manhandling when Rhett did it so famously."

"Well, you are no Rhett Butler!"

He leaned close and whispered in her ear, "And you, my dear, are no Scarlet O'Hara!"

"What's going on here? Do you know where Diana and Claire's Mum are?"

"I know they have young women in there to do the grunt work

but I don't know them by name." He dialed Jock's number and passed his earpiece to Kate.

"Kate? Is that you?"

"Dad? What's going on? Is this secure?"

Charlie bent over and whispered in her ear. "I wouldn't have given it to you if it wasn't!"

Kate ignored him. "I'm in a predicament right now. The head boss thinks I have a sprained ankle so there is no way I can just disappear without causing problems."

"Listen to me! You have to get out of there right now! That place is going to be overrun with DEA. It's going to be the biggest drug bust in the UK in years. Trust Charlie. I'm on my way."

The line disconnected.

They both saw Carter leave the house. He was giving them an odd look.

Charlie waved and pointed to the azalea bushes. He wondered what Carter thought about his sudden interest in flowers.

"We have to move around. The flowers are not that interesting."

Charlie pushed Kate along an ocean path. "I've been working undercover for the past year." Charlie said in a low voice as he pushed her slowly down the ocean path.

"Good grief!" Kate turned in her wheelchair towards him.

"Keep smiling, turn around and point to the boulders down the beach."

Kate did as she was told.

"Don't look now but the Boss is following Carter. They're heading for that big stone building on the water. The story is that he's building fast racing boats in there. Lord James is one of the biggest drug dealers in Europe. I've got to get you out of here. Town officials are coming at noon today to celebrate the new boats. Following that Lord James is hosting a big feast in the castle. They moved up the delivery date to tomorrow.

"That certainly puts a time limit on it. I have to find Diana, my client's girlfriend, and Mary Catherine, Claire's Mum."

Charlie discreetly pocketed the earpiece Kate returned to him. Lord James passed by. Charlie did his best to sound like he was bored to death talking about the waves. When it was safe to talk Charlie asked, "Do you have pictures of the women?"

Kate pulled out her cell and showed him the two pictures she'd downloaded. "Diana has brown hair. Claire's mom is the blonde."

"The blonde was killed in an accident. The other one is still in the building."

"Oh." A sadness touched her heart. "I've got to get Diana out tonight."

"I have an idea." Charlie pushed her back towards the castle.

EIGHTEEN

"What's your idea?"

"When we get inside ask me if I'd take you to town to pick up some female stuff. Make sure Lord James can hear you. Tell me your ankle is a lot better. Say if you can pick up an Ace bandage you can walk around to watch the boats tonight. Once we're in the car don't talk. It's bugged like the house.

"What about the staff?"

"Everyone is involved."

"The housekeeper?"

"Mrs. Callaway, yes. She's married to Carter who is Rocco's right hand man."

"Rocco?" And the footman, Liam?"

"Lord James is really Rocco Mancuso. They keep it in the family. Liam is Carter's son."

"It's like the Mafia."

Charlie went over a rough stone path bumping Kate up and down in the chair. "Ouch."

"It is the Mafia. Lord James is really Rocco, "The Rock." He's from Chicago. He was a Mob Boss until he found a new way of making a lot more money. Then he disappeared and became Lord James. He bought the castle and the title."

"The Rock?"

"He likes to bury people, he's not fond of, under a huge pile of rocks."

Charlie turned and headed back to the castle. "They both saw Lord James and Carter returning from the stone house. At this pace they would meet at the castle.

"Ask to go to town for some lady stuff. Remember the car is bugged so hold any conversation until I tell you we're safe."

"OK." Kate studied Lord James, from under her bowed head, as the two men entered the castle.

They approached the castle so they both stopped talking until they were inside.

"That was lovely, Charlie, thank you. Do you think we might go into town? I need to pick up an Ace bandage and a few things. Would you don't mind taking me?"

"I'll check with Lord James."

Charlie went into the dining room. The door was open so he knew he'd heard Kate's request. Lord James made it a point to know everything that was going on.

He looked up from his paperwork. "I heard. Take her. Having her see the boats tonight is good for business." He smiled.

"Sure enough, Boss. I'll take her to town right away."

"No rush getting back. Delay until we take the boats for a run.

I'd rather she wasn't here any earlier."

"Right."

Charlie went back to where he'd left Kate in the entry. "Ready to go?"

"I am."

Carter brought a new Bentley around to the front door. Charlie got Kate settled into the passenger side while Carter deposited the wheelchair into the boot.

"I'd like to go to a Pharmacy."

"No problem."

That was all they said for the next half hour.

NINETEEN

Jimmy left the main freeway heading for Miami veering off in the direction of Charleston. The narrow streets of the South Carolina town were packed with tourists. Jimmy parked on a side street and was swept into the mob of tourists going up and down the main thoroughfare. He loved being part of a crowd. You could be anonymous. Especially if there was a festival going on: a perfect time to dress in a costume. Halloween in Key West and Mardi Gras and Jazz Fest in New Orleans were his favorites. Actually anytime in the New Orleans French Quarter he could dress in a vampire tour guide costume and fit right in.

He stopped for a snack at one of the charming outdoor cafes on Main Street. He didn't see anyone that caught his interest so he threw a twenty-dollar bill on the table and left. But someone noticed him.

A woman at a table nearby said to her companion. "Sissy, did you see that man at the first table near the street? We passed him coming in."

"I didn't pay attention."

"I did. See the table he's vacating?"

"Yes."

"Right now move to that table and don't let the waiter touch anything. Give him my card. Call Joe. Get gloves and evidence bags here ASAP. I think he's someone I know. I'm just going to catch up with him and say hello."

"No problem." When do you use evidence bags on someone you're saying hello to? But Sissy knew Helen could be a problem, a big problem, for bad guys. Helen was an Assistant District Attorney with ambitions. But one day that instinct of hers was going to get her in trouble.

Helen followed Jimmy 's slow stroll until he turned off busy Main Street onto a leafy, narrow road with charming mansions lining each side of the street.

Jimmy knew he was being followed but he continued his slow walk looking like any of the other thousands of tourists in town.

"Excuse me. Excuse me." Helen fast walked to catch up with him. She wanted a better look at him.

Jimmy turned and feigned surprise that someone was there. "Well hello. Can I help you?"

"I think we met before. Aren't you Ron Littleton?"

"No, sorry. But I don't mind being misidentified by a lovely lady on such a beautiful day. And you are?"

"Melody."

"Then good day to you, Miss Melody."

Helen blushed. "Sorry to bother you." She never forgot a face.

It was Ron Littleton, just a lot older. At the time, he had been a suspect in her sister's murder but he produced an ironclad alibi that ruled him out. After that he disappeared.

Jimmy smiled, turned, and continued on his way. Now they both were lying. He knew who she was. Her name wasn't Melody. It was Helen Powers, an Assistant DA, who could be a real problem. Long ago he had used the name Ron Littleton. He was living in a small town in Arkansas and he had killed a local, Teresa Powers. That was the only time he pursued his hobby, as he liked to call it, in the same town where he was living. He never made that mistake again. But he made sure he had an unshakeable alibi. He heard that Teresa had an older sister whose ambitions had taken her into the field of law. Government law. He remembered seeing her sister sitting near him in the audience, during the trial. She had given him a look of pure hatred even though he was not the one under arrest.

He made sure this time he wasn't being followed when he cut down a side street, doubled back and headed towards his car.

She had ruined his day, of being an unnoticed tourist, and he didn't like that at all. He had to give this situation a lot of thought.

Helen walked slowly back to the cafe. It wouldn't do to see her running but she certainly wanted to.

Joe was at the table with the evidence bags. He and Sissy were putting on gloves before touching anything. Helen joined them.

"Thanks for getting here so fast."

The three were busy carefully putting items into the bags when Jimmy drove, unnoticed, past the cafe.

Jimmy smiled. It was amazing that no one turned to look at what was happening at Table 8 with three people donning sterile gloves, opening evidence bags and putting objects into them. He wished he could be a fly on the wall when Helen got the DNA back and discovered it was in fact Ron Littleton but Ron couldn't be found anymore. Jimmy Landry, his real name, had never submitted his fingerprints or been arrested for anything. So she had nothing. Jimmy laughed and took a right turn leading him to the freeway, and away from Charleston. So Ms. Powers had landed in South Carolina. Charleston, to be exact. He had to remember to take that state off his go-to places for the future which was sad since he had a ticket for Porgy and Bess. The play would be performed in an amphitheater next month. He didn't want to miss it. Maybe he'd do away with Miss Helen before the play. He grinned as he headed for Miami.

TWENTY

"I had no idea you were skilled in riding." Lord Harry rode up behind Claire. "Would you like to see a river where I catch large trout?"

"You fly fish?" Claire smiled. She gently brought Red to a stop.

"Of course. Even if you don't catch anything it's brilliant."

"I would love to see this river."

"Follow me if you can." Harry laughed and spurred his horse to thunder ahead of her.

Claire let him take the lead. There are times a lady should not win and she knew just when those were.

Harry was waiting to help her dismount which was funny since she could outride most men she met. He took her hand and led her to the bank of a meandering river. The water was so clear she could see trout swimming at the bottom, rising occasionally to swallow an insect struggling on the surface.

She was delighted to see a large picnic blanket spread out. One end was filled with silver domed serving dishes and a silver bucket holding a bottle of champagne nestled in crushed ice. A huge tree, with weeping limbs, gave the picnic a very romantic atmosphere.

"Harry, how wonderful!"

"I personally chose the menu."

A small smile creased the side of his cheeks. He had met many women who were more interested in his title and his castle than who he was. A small thing like a picnic would have bored most of them. But not Claire.

She sat down on the blanket with delicate grace. "Look!" She held up a small porcelain tablet with the menu hand written in scroll. She quickly scanned it and smiled. "Everything I love. How did you know?"

"I think Granny has been observing you since you arrived."

"Thank you, Harry!"

He loved the way she tucked into everything in the basket. Finally they both sat with their backs against the huge tree in companionable silence and enjoyed the beautiful afternoon.

"You are the only woman I've met that can sit and enjoy the silence with me."

Claire blushed, hoping he didn't notice.

"I feel like I'm back home in Australia."

"Tell me about your home." He turned his full attention to her.

Claire thought about the sheep and the goats that gave milk and soft cheese that had been gaining in popularity when she left to go to Penzance with her parents.

"My Grandfather has a sheep farm in Australia. I'm expected to take over running it one day."

"I've often thought about raising sheep. We have unused acres but I don't know anything about sheep."

"I do."

"Are you a shepherdess?" He was fascinated.

"No, we have too many sheep. We have Aussie Shepherds and Border Collies that do an excellent job at that. I'm a goat herder!" She laughed. "I love to talk to the goats. They are very sweet. When I left, with my parents, I was just getting into making goat cheese."

The bright blue cloudless sky had gradually been turning into a threatening dark grey color. Now there were ominous sounds of thunder and bright flashes of lightning coming closer and closer.

Harry stood and held out his hand.

They quickly packed the basket with the remains of the picnic.

"Race you back." Harry helped Claire into her saddle and leaped into his but Claire was already racing ahead.

Harry laughed. She can definitely ride!

TWENTY-ONE

Charlie parked down the street from the Pharmacy. Taking his lead Kate waited while he retrieved the wheelchair. They were a distance from the car before he initiated conversation. "Get an Ace bandage and a few personal things."

Kate picked up things that a woman would buy in case Lord James checked the receipts.

At the car he took the bandage out of its wrapping and taped Kate's ankle. He put the wheelchair in the boot and guided her down the street before he finally said anything, "I have an idea. I'll tell you over lunch."

Kate took his arm for support and did a convincing job of strolling slowly as they made their way down a cobblestone path, putting distance from the car behind them.

"I hope you like fish and chips."

"I do."

They arrived at a quaint little outdoor cafe with a big red banner proclaiming Dillon's Fish and Chips, The Best In Scotland.

Charlie made sure Kate was seated. "I'll be right back."

She noticed the man behind the counter nod to Charlie as he went out the back exit. It was a casual nod. If she hadn't been carefully watching, she would have missed it. Charlie was back in exactly ten minutes.

"This is what we're going to do. They test the boats at 1 AM. I'm going to get us back right before Midnight so I can take you right to the stone house. All the women will be asleep. Diana is in a room by herself. You have until Midnight to get Diana and go into the bathrooom, which has a connecting door from Diana's bedroom and one from the dormitory. Be sure and lock all the doors. You don't want anyone coming in until you're safely out of there. There's only one window. Lift it all the way open. There will be men in black wetsuits in a Zodiac in the water below. Send Diana out and then you follow her feet first. They'll take you and Diana to safety."

"What about the guards?"

"The guards will be busy with the fast boats."

"Does Lord James use the boats to transport the drugs?"

"The less you know the better. I'll tell you later. Just do what I tell you."

Kate spent the rest of the afternoon walking around the small village on her newly taped ankle. She liked the old buildings, with shops and outside cafes, lining Main Street.

Charlie kept her away from the castle as long as he could. It was close to Midnight when he brought her to the stone house. After a conversation with the guards Charlie handed her over with a casual wave.

The air had a smell of acid. Kate knew enough about cocaine production to know somewhere in the building they had a workshop.

She turned to the guard who was leading her down a long hallway towards the back of the building. "Thank you for taking me to the woman's barracks."

"No problem. There's a room with an American. I was told to put you in her room until the boats are ready. It might get noisy."

"I understand. Where do I watch the boats?"

"The bathroom has a window that opens. Don't fall out." He laughed. "The water is freezing and you'll be swept to your death by the undertow."

"I'll be careful." Kate smiled.

They came to a dark corridor and walked down to the last door on the right.

The guard stopped. "It's been lights out since ten so everyone's asleep but I think she'll welcome your visit." He opened the door and Kate walked past him.

He shut the door behind her. Diana, who had a hard time sleeping at night, turned on her bedside light. "Who are you?" Diana whispered.

"I'm Kate. And you are...?" She recognized Diana right away.

"Diana."

"I'll call you, Dee. I have a friend, Mike. I call him Mick. I love nicknames, don't you? I'm here to watch the boat races from the bathroom window."

Diana nodded. She knew she could trust Kate.

Diana put her finger to her lips. "I'd love to watch the boat races, too. I'll get dressed."

Diana pulled on her jeans and a sweatshirt. Putting on her Nikes she pointed to the door leading to the bathroom.

The girls went through into a stone bathroom with ten stalls. Kate locked the door behind them and made sure the other doors were locked. Moving quickly she opened the window and looking out she made sure the men were waiting for them below. She indicated to Diana to go out feet first. Just as Kate was ready to follow her, the door flew open and the two guards rushed in. One had a handgun outfitted with a silencer pointed right at her.

"Hi, Guys, nice night out, doncha think?"

She found the elongated muzzle pressed between her breasts, pushing her further into the room. She knew the proximity was meant to intimidate her so she put a helpless and horrified look on her face as she quickened her steps backward, forcing her antagonist to move with her. She quickly looked over his shoulder to see if the second man had drawn a gun. He had his hand at the fold of his jacket but had not actually drawn a weapon.

Raising her shaking hands just above the level of the handgun pressing into her chest, she started to bleat, "Please, no, I…" then softly slid the back of her right hand along the right side the gun barrel as she turned her hips clockwise. The gunmen could feel no touch on his hand but found that he was suddenly aiming at the wall, Kate having slipped to his right. She reversed her right hand to grip the barrel and trigger guard, knowing that any movement might result in a discharge of the weapon. But she had to move before he righted himself. Her left palm-heel struck the inside of his right wrist, opening his grip. As his hand lost his grip on the weapon, his forefinger grazed the trigger, a round went off, and the recoil of the slide scraped Kate's hand along the barrel, the ejecting cartridge burning the outside edge of her palm. Through force of will she retained hold of the weapon slamming the grip into the neck of the gunman. His head arched backward as she transferred the pistol to her left hand. Over the shoulder of her antagonist, she could see the second man drawing his gun. She arched her right arm around the man she had disarmed and sacrificed her standing position to clothesline him to the floor. She rolled over his chest and did her best to aim toward the second gunman from a kneeling position.

The second man readjusted his aim on her new position as she reached her weapon toward him. Suddenly, he arched forward, chest first. Behind him stood Charlie, his right front kick pulling back to the floor.

Rolling on the floor, the man turned to his new target, but Charlie pounced, his left knee landing on the gunman's right forearm, his left jaw taking the force of Charlie's punch.

Kate turned her weapon on the first gunman, making sure not to get close enough so he could touch any part of the pistol. "I don't suppose there's any duct tape around here. Use the pillowcases. They'll have to do."

Charlie smiled at Kate. "Bind them, gag them, and…?"

"How about a utility closet?"

"A utility closet it is."

They wound four of them into cords that would create a stronger cincture and a more uncomfortable gag.

"Why did you come back?"

"I wanted to make sure you were okay."

A softness Kate had never seen before came into his eyes. It was at that moment they connected. That indefinable moment when Kate looked at Charlie like he was a man. She wanted to put her arms around his well-defined body, rest her head on his chest for a while, run her fingers though straight, dark unruly hair that fell across his forehead. The kind of thing that irritates a man to no end but they smile and tolerate it just because. She could get lost in his dark blue eyes and smile when she could hear him saying he wanted to know about her, everything about her. But the contact between them was broken when one of the rescue team, all wearing black wetsuits, swept

her up and handed her out the window to the waiting support of the

men still in the Zodiak. Diana was sitting in the stern in a warm jacket

thoughtfully provided by the agents. She held up a jacket for Kate.

Looking up at the empty window Kate could still feel the warmth that

had flooded her body looking at Charlie for that moment.

She sat next to Diana and put on the oversized coat.   Boats and

men were landing up and down the beach. The drug bust had begun.

Without a word one of their rescuers started up the engine and headed

for the open body of water leading to the Irish Sea.

Wind battered their faces so talking was impossible. Kate

realized she had lost her cell phone. When they were no longer in sight

of the lights on the beach they pulled up to the side of a massive cargo

ship. The girls were ushered up the side on a rope ladder. While Diana

was given hot coffee and blankets Kate went inside below deck to use

the ships phone. She called her client, Mike Greenwald. He answered

right away.

"Mr. Greenwald, this is Kate Bodine. I have Diana with me."

"Kate, I can't thank you enough. Your father called and has kept

me up to date. I've been so worried. Where are you?"

"We're on our way to Greystone Abbey. It's my Granny's house.

Can you meet us there?"

"Of course. Can I talk to Diana?"

"We're on a big cargo ship. I left her above deck to call you."

"I'm leaving right now. Tell her I can't wait to see her."

"I will."

TWENTY-TWO

Kate returned to find Diana watching a helicopter land on the deck of the cargo ship.

Diana frantically waved her over. "They're taking us to England."

The two girls rushed to board, bending down to avoid the whirling propellers. Kate had to yell over the noise. She kept her conversation clipped. "I called Mike Greenwald. He hired me to find you. He said he'd meet us in England."

To Kate's surprise her Dad got out of the helicopter to help Diana get in.

Before they parted Diana touched Kate's arm. There was too much noise to talk but her eyes said it all. Seconds later Diana disappeared inside the cockpit.

Jock gave his daughter a big hug. "Beans, thank God! I'll see you at the Big House."

Kate giggled and hugged him back. She felt like a young girl when he called her Beans. He'd given her that nickname because of her love of Louisiana Monday night dinners of Red Beans and Rice, a New Orleans tradition. And he called Greystone Abbey, The Big House, knowing it would make her smile. Louisiana had plantations, but not castles, so to avoid confusion he'd told everyone Kate's Granny had a Big House.

He helped her into the cockpit and jumped back to the deck of the cargo ship before the helicopter lifted up, banked sharply and disappeared into a cloud bank. Flashing lights, two way conversations, back and forth, on hand held radios, wind from the helicopter blades, heavy rain and choppy seas all made any conversation impossible. The girls huddled together. Kate brought Diana up to date with everything she knew. After that sleep was not an option it was inevitable.

Kate woke up to a fast descent in front of Greystone Abbey.

The helicopter gently touched down.

They could see Harry and Claire coming out of Greystone Abbey to greet them. Granny followed with her cane.

Diana whispered to Kate. "Please let me tell Claire about her Mum. We were great friends. I was with her at the end."

Kate nodded. She knew Claire would be looking for her Mum.

Granny hovered over Kate like a Mother Hen. She knew what had happened. Jock had kept her up to date on the action.

Claire rushed to hug Diana. Kate gave the two girls privacy and went into the house holding Granny's arm. Harry hung back offering support if needed. Kate knew by the gentle look he gave Claire that they had formed a close bond. It made her sad when she thought about Charlie. Would he ever look at her like that? She shook off the thought. He was a Mercenary, off on another job after this one.

Granny led her into the Drawing Room. She sat on a small sofa next to Granny and told her the whole story. When she talked about Charlie her voice quivered. It was enough for someone as astute as Granny to know this was someone important in her Granddaughters life.

"My darling, Kate, is Charlie the one who is making you sad right now?"

"Yes. Kate whispered. I don't think I'll ever see him again."

"He must be very special."

"He is."

An idea came to Granny. She smiled. "I am happy to have you back safe. How long can you stay with me?"

"Just a few days but I promise I will be back soon for a very long visit."

Dawson opened the door and inquired "Would you like tea, Mi'Lady?"

"That would be lovely."

He closed the door behind him and hurried to give orders to the kitchen staff.

At that moment Claire and Harry joined them in the Drawing Room.

Granny noticed the way Harry held his arm around Claire in

her delicate state. "Dawson is bringing tea. And your friend, Diana?"

"She just heard from Mike Greenwald. He should be here soon."

Kate noticed that Granny was smiling, something she did not

do that often. She had no idea Granny was such a romantic.

At that moment Dawson held the door open and Eric, the first

footman entered carrying a large silver tray filled with everything for a

proper tea. He placed it on the delicate Regency table in front of the sofa.

Hearing the sound of a helicopter overhead Kate moved to

the window. She recognized Mike Greenwald getting out of a fast,

streamlined black helicopter with his Omega Corporation logo on the

side. Mike swept Diana off her feet. She thought about Charlie. She

hadn't felt this alone since Peter died.

She went back and whispered to Granny, "Mike arrived.

They're having a reunion right now." She went back to the window.

Claire and Harry, Diana and Mike. It was too much to bear right now.

Tears silently slid down her cheeks. Only Granny knew by the slight lift

of her shoulders that she was very sad. It was that way when her Mum

died. She never let anyone see her cry, but Granny knew.

Granny called to Kate. "Come sit by me."

Diana and Mike joined the group. They were holding hands.

Everyone smiled, even Kate forgot her sadness.

"I can't thank you enough." Mike smiled.

Kate wished Charlie had smiled at her like Mike did with

Diana. Instead all Charlie had done was give her orders and look unhappy with everything she did.

"Kate, I owe you---"

"---You owe me nothing. I just did my job."

She made a mental note to return the advance check he'd given her. It was way over her expenses.

She noticed Granny had been talking to Diana and Mike. The sound of the rotors started up outside. They made their goodbyes. Kate watched them run to the waiting helicopter. They took off and banked right, flattening the green lawn in front of the castle.

Claire poured tea. She and Harry sat and talked to Granny for a while before leaving to stroll through the gardens.

Kate turned from the window. "Granny, did you hear from Dad?"

"I did. He called right before you arrived. He said the action was over and he'd see you back home."

"He's not coming here?" She sat beside Granny.

"He had loose ends to tie up. That's what he said."

"I understand."

"Your things were retrieved from Scotland and brought here a few hours ago. I put everything in your room."

"Oh, Granny, thank you. I could do with a bath and a change of clothes before dinner."

"Things have been so rushed I didn't have time to tell you the good news." Granny smiled.

"Would it have to do with the engagement ring I saw Claire wearing?"

"Yes. She and Harry are getting married."

"Soon?"

"I don't know. There's so much to do. I also have another surprise. Wally and her husband are arriving tomorrow. I can't wait to see her and I think it will be wonderful for Claire. And with the engagement it comes at a perfect time."

"Granny, I am happy for you, too. She was your friend from boarding school. I will keep your surprise a secret."

"I know you will. You are so much like your Mum."

Thinking of her Mum was very sad. Every time she visited Granny she took a boat over to the island and visited her Mum's resting place. She would go there first thing in the morning.

Kate kissed Granny on the cheek and left the room, leaving Granny deep in thought about her wonderful memories of days at boarding school with her dear friend.

Kate ascended the grand staircase and thought about the time Charlie had gallantly carried her to her bedroom in Lord James' manor house. She shook her head like she could shake away any memory of him. If it was only that easy, she thought. After a hot bath she unpacked her clothes. Checking her watch she realized it was almost time for dinner.

TWENTY-THREE

Dinner was a very quiet affair with everyone lost in their own thoughts. One bright moment was when she congratulated Claire on her engagement. But then things turned somber again. What girl doesn't want her Mum there to be by her side at such a time?

Kate was totally exhausted so when Granny suggested she go to bed early Kate gratefully took the suggestion.

She climbed into her Renaissance four poster tester bed and drew the dark green velvet curtains around the sides. She didn't want to be disturbed by the early morning light that would pour through the windows.

It was just daybreak when she woke up the next morning. She'd dreamed about Mum jumping her horse. The dream stopped just short where the horse refused a jump and her Mum fell head first onto the unforgiving ground.

Kate dressed quickly and paddled a canoe to the island where all the Sanfords lay in caskets inside an ornately carved marble mausoleum. Just as she arrived the sky was turning a light blue with clouds thin and wispy. It was, all in all, turning out to be a beautiful day. Kate secured a rope from the canoe to the dock. She loved the walk down the well worn grass path. Birds were chirping, butterflies were flitting around. Such a contrast to the sadness the place evoked in her. Both her Grandfather and her Mum were entombed here.

Kate entered the six number combination in the heavy steel door and listened for the reassuring clicks before it creaked open. There were marble benches, held up by lion heads, scattered around the huge room. A small pink rosebud was in the vase attached to her Mum's tomb. A white azalea was blooming in profusion on top of Grandfather's tomb. A skylight overhead kept a constant beam of morning light directed on the flowering plant.

Sitting on a marble bench next to her Mum's resting place Kate spoke in a quiet, broken voice. She could almost feel the touch of her Mum's hand on her shoulder.

Before she left she had a few minutes with her Grandfather. She missed him dearly.

Rowing back she decided she would leave her sadness behind and look to the future. She had cried her last tear for Peter. Her heart was open for what may lay ahead.

Kate stood on the path surrounded by dense forest and watched as Thomas, their gamekeeper, was pulling up in Granny's stately Rolls. A woman, who Kate knew at a glance had to be Wally, was having a joyful reunion with Granny. Wally's husband was tall and imposing. He must have been tired as his step was nowhere near as sprightly as Wally. He leaned heavily on a cane. Kate smiled.

Claire and Harry appeared from inside. The girl rushed into her Grandmother's arms.

Granny led Wally's husband inside.

Kate was glad no one had noticed her. She felt like an intruder. This was a time for their reunions. She decided to leave for New Orleans as soon as possible. She would return in a few months closer to the time of the wedding. She made a mental note to look for her cell phone so she could make plane reservations. Then she remembered. Her phone had disappeared during the fight with the guards in the stone house bathroom.

Kate put a smile on her face, and a spring in her step, as she went in search of Granny. She didn't have to go far as voices were coming from the dining room. She hadn't had breakfast. Her smile was genuine when she met Claire's Grandparents. They were delightful.

Eric served one enticing dish after another. The marble topped buffet was filled with everything anyone could want.

It was at the end of breakfast that Kate told Granny she was leaving for New Orleans. She knew there was an overnight train at the village station getting into Paddington first thing in the morning. Then a flight from Heathrow later that day. She'd taken the same train many times.

Granny tried but couldn't talk her out of leaving so she told her how much she would be missed.

Kate smiled and told her she would be back for a visit very soon.

After saying goodbye to everyone she went into the library to use the phone to make plane reservations for the next day.

Eric put her valise into the boot of the Rolls. It seemed like everyone came outside to see her leave. She kept up a brave face, smiling and waving back. Harry and Claire, Granny and Wally and somewhere Diana and Mike. It was all too much. She vowed to stop feeling sorry for herself.

She was happy, yet sad, to leave the country of her birth behind her. Sad because everyone had someone to love but not her and happy because being there reminded her of Scotland and Charlie Campbell.

Watson had the cook pack sandwiches, a variety of cheese and a wonderful bottle of wine. The stewart assigned to her cabin, at her request, turned down her bed early, leaving sweets on her pillow. Kate fell asleep quite early and woke as the train was pulling into Paddington in the morning. She quickly tided up and caught a taxi for Heathrow soon after.

She retrieved her old Land Rover from long term parking at the New Orleans Airport and drove straight to her houseboat in the bayou. It was the only place where she would find peace right now. She had taken an entire day to decide what she wanted to paint the houseboat, ten years ago, when she'd first purchased it. She loved the soft coral color with turquoise trim. It reminded her of the shotgun houses in the French Quarter so named because it was said you could open the front door and shoot a shotgun straight through to the back yard. One room opened to another by a long hallway.

The minute her foot touched the wide board, leading from land to her houseboat, she heard a loud hissing. Fred, ever vigilant, was earning his dinner. Kate laughed. "Fred, you're the best alarm chicken parts can buy." She threw a whole raw chicken towards the ten foot, four hundred pound alligator who snatched it in mid air and slithered off the front porch into the dark green water. The houseboat rocked gently.

Kate spent the next few days cleaning. She loved the cozy interior with shabby chic overstuffed chairs, sink-into sofas and her favorite was the 1950's chrome table with a white Formica top kitchen table and chrome chairs with red vinyl seats. Her kitchen was right out of the 50's with Turquoise painted appliances. Her bedroom was at the very back of the houseboat surrounded by glass. She had painted the front and back door grey blue, which she found very relaxing. When it stormed she opened all the curtains and felt like she was in the middle of the rainstorm, only safe and sound. It was the night of the fourth day home, she had just started a fire in the dark grey Vermont Casting fireplace when she heard a huge commotion of Fred hissing and her Dad yelling outside.

She looked out the window and saw Fred moving in a very menacing way down the gangplank towards her Dad who had been quickly backing up. "I've been worried about you!" He yelled over the commotion.

Kate opened the window and yelled. "Fred, you are being a bad boy! Leave my Dad alone! Go for a swim!"

Jock could swear that the alligator swung his head towards Kate and actually looked ashamed that he had made her angry. Then Fred slid off the boardwalk making a huge splash into the water, splashing her Dad with bayou water, in the process. He made a face.

Kate opened her door and stood there laughing. She handed her Dad a towel. "I don't think you have to worry about me. I have a terrific bodyguard."

He moped off his face and grumbled. "Do you know your phone is turned off?"

"That's because I don't know where it is. I lost it somewhere." Why did he have to remind her of the stone house and Charlie?

"Granny has been trying to reach you." Jock sat down in her favorite overstuffed chair near the fireplace.

"Anything serious?" Kate was alarmed.

"Only if you call two people getting married serious." He smiled.

"Harry and Claire?" She was overjoyed at the news.

"Yep. And Claire wants you to be her Maid of Honor. How soon do you think you can get The Big House? There's a lot to do."

"This is so sudden."

"Not really. You knew she was engaged but then everything speeded up when Claire found out her Grandfather was seriously ill. That's why they made the trip from Australia. He insisted that he wanted to give her away."

Kate remembered she thought he'd looked tired but now she understood.

"I can go right now. Well, after I make a plane reservation. You're going with me, right?"

He got up and walked to the door. "I can't. I'm busy but I'll be there as soon as I finish. You need to be there now." He looked out the window. "Beans, is that Louisiana yard dog waiting to take a bite out of me?"

Kate sighed. Her Dad was so big and strong. She didn't think anything unnerved him, until he'd ran into Fred.

"Want me to walk you to your car, Dad?"

"No thanks!" He stopped, pulled a flip cell phone out of his pocket and handed it to her. "Use this until you get a new one. It's a secure line. If I had been able to call you I would have. Now I can." He handed her a piece of paper. "Memorize the number and toss it."

"Thanks, Dad. I know the routine." Kate stood on her front porch and watched her Dad walk, with a quick step, down the plank towards his car parked on land. She smiled when he looked over his shoulder, once or twice, thinking maybe Fred was stalking him.

TWENTY-FOUR

Jimmy Landry was people watching, a favorite pastime, at a New Orleans airport cafe when he thought about the past week. It had been a total success. He'd sold a one hundred foot yacht to a client in Houston. Usually he had a crew deliver the yachts but this time he decided to motor it himself. On the way he stopped in Charleston and dealt with Helen Powers, an Assistant District Attorney, who would never fulfill her ambitions of a higher political position with her body resting somewhere on the bottom of the Gulf of Mexico, food for all the bottom feeders. She had spoiled his visit to Charleston on a lovely sunny afternoon after a delightful lunch at an outdoor cafe. He had vowed to make her pay for that. He did.

After delivering the yacht in Houston he was on him way back to Miami when he had a long layover in New Orleans.

He added way too much sugar to his Cafe au Lait and scanned the people walking by from his seat at a huge window. Airports were like the streets of Mardi Gras and Jazz Fest, all filled with lots of women traveling alone. Many from somewhere else. Many who might not be missed for a while. It said something. One stood out in the crowd. Tall, blonde, alone. But he'd seen her somewhere. He threw a twenty on the table and followed her. He remembered as he walked. She had

been in a photo with Sarah inside the girl's bookstore in Cross Creek.

Walking next to her he said "I've seen you before."

Kate spoke as she walked, "Really where?" She gave him a

sideways glance. Tall, handsome, interesting.

"In Sarah's bookstore in Cross Creek. You and Sarah were in a

frame on a small table by the sofa."

Kate stopped. "You're the school friend who gave her concert

tickets."

"I am."

"I had to drive to Cross Creek in the middle of the night and

solve the problem of just where Sarah had gone. You should have left a

calling card."

Jimmy smiled. "I would have signed it, Jimmy Landry. Would

the tall, bonde girl who finds this card have dinner with me?"

"I have a plane to catch." He was definitely charming. She

noticed how women, walking by, turned to look at him.

"I do, too, but there's always another one to Miami."

"What do you do that allows you to commute when you want?"

"I'm a Treasure Hunter."

"Really!" She was definitely interested. Kate had a secret desire

to dive on sunken pirate ships since she'd read Treasure Island.

Jimmy laughed. "On weekends. The rest of the time I sell

boats. Have you heard of Marcella Boats?"

"Those aren't boats. Those are hundred foot yachts."

"That they are."

"Well, good for you but I'm going to my cousin's wedding in England and I have a flight to catch." She liked everything about him. He was wearing a dark suit, and a tie, loose at the neck. His blonde streaked hair was just a bit too long. She bet there were many women who would love to run their fingers through it. She wasn't one of them. She couldn't get Charlie Campbell out of her mind.

"Another time?"

"I would love to. Give me your cell number and I'll call you when I get back." She remembered her Aunt saying how kind he was to Sarah. Maybe she would call him back.

She handed him a paper and pen. She slipped it into the pocket of her jacket.

"I don't think I got your name." She was hard to get. He loved that!

"I don't think I gave it." She walked off in the direction of the international terminal. She looked back and smiled at him.

At that moment Jimmy felt something he'd never felt before, intense interest in a woman that had nothing to do with what usually turned him on. He couldn't wait until she returned.

TWENTY-FIVE

When she arrived at the train station in Fowey she was happy to see Thomas waiting next to Granny's Rolls. She expected Eric so things must be very busy at the castle. She had tons of questions to ask the head gamekeeper about the upcoming wedding but he told her he had been too busy supplying Greystone with venison from the forests and fish from their private lake to notice anything else.

Kate fell asleep. She felt the car coming to a stop and a deep voice saying her name. "Kate, or is it Sleeping Beauty?"

He sounded so much like Charlie! She wanted to see him so bad she had started to hear his voice in her dreams.

The car door opened. She expected to see Thomas instead of Charlie Campbell! He quirked up one eyebrow that was charming and inquiring at the same time, something he could do so well.

"Oh, it's you!" Kate frowned at him.

"Aww, and here I thought the Queen was arriving."

"What are you doing here, Charlie?"

"No hi, how are you, good to see you?" Charlie grinned. "No? Well, I'm here for the wedding. And you are a bit late getting here, aren't you? Must be the bayou air!"

"Harry and Claire?" Kate couldn't have looked more surprised. She ignored his criticism.

"I don't know anyone else getting married in a few days, do you?"

"You know Harry?"

"I do."

"Why didn't you tell me you knew him?"

"If I recall you were very busy saving the world and I had no idea Harry was your cousin and would be getting married."

"Pray tell, just how do you know Harry?"

"We went to Oxford together."

"You were the Yank friend he talked about?" Kate felt her mouth drop open. She shut it with a snap.

"In the flesh." Charlie made a gallant gesture and held out his hand to help her out of the car.

She recoiled like she was confronted by a King Cobra. She wanted to say...Why didn't you call me? Why didn't you---?

He broke into her thoughts almost like he knew what she was thinking. "You can't be mad at me forever. After all I'm going to be Harry's Best Man! Do you need a wheelchair or has your ankle healed?" He grinned. "Last time I saw you it looked okay."

Embarrassed that he was so in tune to her thoughts she blushed and yet growled at the same time. "I don't need your help." She lifted her chin in an uncharacteristically haughty manner. "I'm perfectly capable of exiting a car by myself." She knocked away his hand and stomped on his toes getting out. Wearing leather Nikes didn't do as much harm as she wished.

Charlie backed up and hoped on one foot.

Oh, the drama! She thought. She glared at him. "Cut it out!"

"I'm really hurt." He smiled and then moved aside so that she saw almost everyone was standing outside awaiting her arrival. And they all had seen the exchange between them.

Granny had a lace handkerchief to her forehead looking like she was going to faint. Harry and Claire looked amused. Claire's Grandparents, Wally and her husband, leaning on a cane, were trying not to look distressed. The staff were lined up like she was visiting royalty and, except for a few giggles, were looking down at their feet trying desperately to appear like they hadn't seen Lady Kate, in a tiff, stomping on Charlie Campbell's foot. They all thought he was one of the nicest Yanks they had ever met.

Charlie took her arm pretending like they were great friends. "We're going to be seeing a lot of each other...Best Man, Maid of Honor sort of thing."

With a big smile on her face Kate said through clenched teeth. "You are insufferable!"

"I've been called worse." He patted her arm soothingly. "Now try to be good. He almost liked it when she was acting crazy!

They strolled up to the waiting crowd followed by Thomas pulling Kate's rolling luggage.

Kate hugged Granny and whispered "I am so happy to be home. Charlie and I were just having a bit of fun. No harm done."

Granny looked her in the eye. She knew her Granddaughter well. "I hope that's true, Katie. I think he's a nice young man."

Kate thanked everyone for the wonderful welcoming reception. She noticed Granny took Charlie's arm and they headed inside. Kate watched them and fumed. Imagine that! Granny giving some...some... stranger her time instead of her own Granddaughter! Well, she sighed, it gave her a chance to talk to Claire. The two girls walked off for a private chat.

"How long has he been here?" Kate was so distressed she wanted to cry and laugh at the same time. They sat on a wide wooden bench under a draping oak tree that shaded them from view.

"For a week. Everyone loves him."

"Ohhh." Kate couldn't believe she had been so selfish thinking only of herself. "Have you been okay?"

Claire whispered to keep tears at bay. "I'm glad it's all over and now I know what happened to my Mum. Harry has been so supportive."

"Did they get Billy Flynn and his band of thieves?"

"They were all taken into custody except for that Gypsy mafia guy."

"I remember...his name was Roman."

"He disappeared."

"They'll find him." As she said that she had a strange feeling

someone was watching her. Changing the subject she said "I'm sorry I
didn't get the message about the wedding until two days ago."

"I was really worried. We tried to reach you and finally Granny
called your Dad."

"I have a hideout in the bayou. I was there and didn't have a
phone. I lost my cell somewhere in Scotland."

"You are my only friend. I wanted you to be my Maid of Honor
so Harry finally reached your Dad. He knew where you might be."

"Thank you for waiting for me. And I am thrilled for you.
Harry is a wonderful guy."

"I don't know what I would have done without him."

"And what a surprise seeing Charlie here. I didn't know you
knew him." Why couldn't she stop talking about Charlie? Stop it right
now! She commanded herself.

"Well, I didn't, and then he was here. Harry told me they've
been friends for years."

"My, my, small world." Kate brushed an irritating bee from
her face. She was ready to change the subject of Charlie Campbell but
Claire looked like she was just getting started.

"Charlie is really amazing. Do you know he grew up on a
ranch?"

"Really? Maybe we should go inside. It looks like a storm is
headed this way."

"I don't see any hint of a storm." Claire arched her head in a graceful manner that Kate wished she could do. "Anyway. The ranch was an orphanage."

"What?" It was Kate's turn to arch her neck but she was sure she looked more like a giraffe instead of a swan. She was glad Charlie wasn't around to see how very ungraceful she could be.

"He lost his parents when he was quite young and there was no one to take care of him. He was placed in a state run orphanage near Boston. He studied very hard and made incredible grades that earned him scholarships everywhere."

"So that's how he got to Oxford."

"Yes. Harry admires him greatly."

Kate desperately wanted to stop the Charlie Campbell adoration so she jumped up and changed the subject. "I'd love to go visit Red. Have you been riding him every day?"

"I have. He's very gentle. Charlie rides, too."

Kate wanted to ask just which horse he was riding but that would have brought them back to the same subject.

Claire just continued talking as they walked across the back lawn towards the red brick stables. "Charlie has been riding Thunder."

"What?" Kate stopped walking. "Nobody can ride Thunder. He's wild. Only my Grandfather could ride him."

"Well now he's been tamed." Claire stopped to pick a wildflower.

"Oh, now he's also a horse whisperer!"

"What did you say?"

"Nothing. Such a talented man, Charlie is."

The two girls walked arm in arm to the stables. Kate asked Eric, the stable boy, for a carrot and fed it to Red. The magnificent horse hadn't forgotten her. He put his soft mouth in her hand. She whispered in his ear. "At least someone appreciates me."

Harry finally joined them. He suggested they all go for a ride before tea.

Kate loved the idea. She had been sitting in, as they say, trains, planes and automobiles for hours!

"I have to change." Claire announced. It was true. Claire was a girly girl and Kate admired her greatly for that.

"I'm fine like this." Kate was wearing a navy blazer, jeans, t-shirt and the now famous "I stepped on his toes, black leather Nikes."

Harry took Claire's arm and said over his shoulder, as they headed back to the Big House, "If you see to Eric saddling the horses I'll get Charlie to join us."

"Oh, wow, that sounds like so much fun!" Kate turned away before she screamed.

As soon as they were out of sight she marched into the stables and called for Eric. She had him saddle Red, Ronan, Thunder and a small little mare that moved at a snail's pace but had beautiful foals, just perfect for Charlie, she thought with a grin.

"Eric, take all the horse to the front of the house except for Thunder. I'll take him myself."

The stable hand looked skeptical of Lady Kate's order but he liked her a lot and if that's what she wanted okay then.

Kate watched Eric lead the three horses away. She spoke lovingly to Thunder. It was mainly to get her incredible terror about riding him under control. After all, she reasoned, she grew up riding horses and if Charlie could ride Thunder, so could she! She'd show him a thing or two about taming a wild horse.

Kate stood on a tree stump she used when she was little. Thunder was a big horse! The minute she swung her foot across the saddle and seated herself she realized this was the worst decision of her life. Thunder shot out of the stable area like a rocket ship. Kate desperately looked for a horn to grab on to like Western saddles but this was an English saddle. She was out of luck. Reins in one hand she grabbed Thunder's flowing mane with the other hand. Thunder raced past the stunned group assembled in front of the house.

Claire screamed.

Harry shouted "What not!"

Charlie jumped on Red and raced after Kate. Thunder had his ears back, his tail up and he was racing like the Beast from Hell was after him. Charlie was determined to catch Thunder before he came to the first jump of the Fox Hunt they held once a year.

TWENTY-SIX

Pulling alongside Thunder, Charlie reached over and grabbed Kate by the waist and hauled her over his saddle like a bag of flour. Kate's face was beet red with embarrassment. Slowly Charlie got Red under control and they came to a canter that bounced Kate up and down. "You need a good spanking!"

"Don't you dare!"

He came to a stop. "I wouldn't think of it. Granny has been through enough for one day!" Before Kate could say anything else he said "Would you like to ride behind me like a Lady?"

"Yes." Kate mumbled in abject humiliation.

"I didn't hear you."

"YES!" I said YES!"

"You don't need to get testy. A simple yes, thank you, would do."

"I don't intend to speak to you ever again."

"That's going to make serving as Maid of Honor and Best Man really difficult."

"I'll extend it until after the ceremony."

"Sounds reasonable." Charlie laughed. Oh, yes, she was definitely more interesting when she was acting crazy.

They trotted up to the waiting group that now included everyone from Granny to the kitchen scullery maid. Everyone looked petrified except Harry. He had a big smile on his face. Kate may have grown up riding but so had Charlie on a ranch.

Kate slid off Red's rump and dusted herself off. "Thank you. Let's all go back inside. Things are well under control. "

Charlie got off Red like a man born in the saddle.

At that moment Thunder raced by still looking terrified at the sight of Kate and headed back to the stables. The other three horses took off, following dutifully behind him, their reins trailing on the ground.

Granny took Charlie's arm dying to hear all the details.

"Well, that's cozy!" She huffed as she watched Granny and Charlie walk off. She took Claire's arm. "I'm sorry I spoiled our ride today. Maybe another day, another horse."

Tea was memorable with Kate managing not to look at or speak to Charlie.

Claire suggested they go upstairs to look at Kate's Maid of Honor dress. Fortunately she had a wardrobe of Kate's clothes to research for size and Granny told her Kate's favorite color was light blue.

The girls had a grand time gossiping and trying on clothes until dinner. At seven sharp Charlie knocked on Kate's door, stuck his head in and informed them, "Dinner is served."

Thankfully Kate was seated next to Wally on her left and Claire on her right. Wally filled in all the stories Granny hadn't told her about their school days. Kate and Claire had a wonderful time. Charlie was seated across the table from Kate between Harry and John, Claire's grandfather. Every now and then he glanced at Kate. When their eyes met Kate looked away. She was still mortified over what had happened earlier.

Kate didn't eat much of the wonderful meal. She had a headache. Making her excuses she went up to bed right after. She took two aspirin and hoped the headache would go away before morning. It did go away after a few hours and now her appetite returned. Laying there debating what to do there was a knock on the door. When she opened it she found a small tray with a sandwich and a warm cup of milk on a table in the hall next to her room. She smiled. And here she thought Granny had forgotten her.

Then she saw Charlie opening his door down the hall. He looked back and waved. She grabbed the tray and kicked the door shut behind her. She certainly wasn't going to be bought off with a sandwich and milk. She was still angry with him. She pulled the napkin off the tray and there sat her cell phone, the one that she had lost. She flipped it open. Her phone was dead. It definitely needed a charge. She was glad she had the backup cell her Dad had given her. In spite of herself she smiled. Thoughts of Charlie filled her head.

The warm milk put her right to sleep.

The next morning she woke up with sunlight pouring through a floor to ceiling leaded mullioned window. The wedding ceremony was going to be held tomorrow morning in the Chapel on the Castle

grounds. For generations all the Sanfords had been married there.

She recalled Claire saying something about the four of them going to

dinner at the local pub tonight. Well, chin up, she'd stick it out for just

this night. After the wedding she would avoid him. But why did the

thought make her sad? She had to admit she felt alive whenever he was

around. She remembered sitting behind him on that horse. So close.

She could smell the essence of him. His back was strong and warm.

Little tingling sensations covered her body like Goosebumps. She

snuggled under her comforter and then realized "What in the world

was she thinking of? Charlie Campbell was bad for her health."

She leaped up and ran a tub of hot water and as she washed her

hair, sitting in the tub, she remembered the song "She had to wash that

man right out of her hair and send him on his way!" But there was

no joy in that thought. What was happening to her? She left her hair

long and hanging down her back with the slightest of curls around her

face. Usually she wore it in a ponytail or a braid over her left shoulder

but tonight was special. She was going out to an intimate dinner and

Charlie was going to be there.

She was too late for breakfast but the cook made sure she had

put a plate in the warmer for her. She sat there eating alone thinking

about the upcoming dinner with Charlie, Claire and Harry tonight.

Actually she was looking forward to it. Good manners said she had to

thank him for finding and returning her cell phone.

With Harry and Charlie nowhere around she spent the day with

Claire going over the flower arrangements, last minute decisions about

the cake that was almost finished, and then Claire surprised her with

a big announcement. Her Grandfather had turned over the running

of the farm in Australia to her. The biggest assets were the twenty

thousand black face sheep that grazed on their land. Five years ago the

Queen had visited Darwin and made the sheep raised at Harris Farm

the official lamb that would grace her dinner table. Being awarded

the official Queens' shield was an enormous honor. There was no way

Harry could leave England so Claire brought all the sheep here to the

Castle's grazing land.

Claire took her to the Chapel and ran through what was

expected of her as the Maid of Honor.

When they finished Kate had just enough time to change into

a dark blue silk pants suit and meet Harry, Claire and Charlie in the

Drawing Room prior to leaving for the pub.

It was a short drive to The Roaring Lion, an old English pub,

outside of Fowey.

Before the meal the guys ordered drinks. Kate and Claire had a

glass of white wine.

Dinner was a very quiet affair with everyone lost in his own

thoughts. One bright moment was when she again congratulated Claire

on her upcoming marriage. But then things turned very quiet again.

Kate got things going when she told Claire about the boys

driving Lord James' car into the fountain. They all started laughing.

Claire excused herself and headed to the loo in the back of the pub.

Kate made a quick decision to follow her.

Charlie watched Kate walk away. She was the type of woman he had always...Kate's scream snapped his reverie.

Pushing his chair behind him, Charlie raced towards the loo, Harry only steps behind him.

A heavy, bearded man in dark slacks and sports jacket had taken Kate by the hair and was pulling her out a rear exit. She was squeezing both hands down on his thick fist, which was nearly the width of her head, in order to diminish his control, but her weight and lack of stability was nearly inconsequential against his strength and traction as he backed toward the door. She could not open his grip but was fighting her extrication by delivering off-balanced kicks to his shins and knees.

As the big man began to fill the exit, Charlie could see past his side that Claire was being strong-armed, a cloth over her nose and mouth, towards a van that was only yards from the doorway. It was Roman, the gypsy guy that Kate had described. He yelled to Harry to rush to the back of the pub.

Kate stomped on the large man's instep before he swung her by the hair into the hand dryer on the wall. The dryer began blowing air spitting red specks into the loo. A line of blood formed on her forehead as she fell to the tile floor her, her assailant now Charlie's assailant.

In the pub the guests turned in their seats at the sound of the commotion several of them getting up, and three beginning to walk towards the loo, only to hear something or someone slam against the door from the inside.

As Charlie circled to his right, Kate's attacker did the same, leaving the rear entrance open. Two more men, both in dark turtlenecks, pushed through the opening. Charlie glimpsed Roman tossing an unconscious Clair into the rear of the van. Casting aside the wet cloth, Roman aimed back towards the doorway.

Kate, unable to see Roman, waited until all three men backed Charlie against the doorway to the pub. She then took several large steps toward the right rear of the outermost man and swung a low left roundhouse kick into the back of his leg, forcing him to fall heavily on one knee to the hard tile. She immediately followed up with a right roundhouse kick toward the left side of his neck, collapsing left jugular vein and carotid artery, instantly rendering him unconscious, at least for a while. He froze for a moment on one knee before falling to the floor. The bearded man turned long enough to allow Charlie an opening. A sudden front kick to the groin folded the big man low enough so that Charlie could swing his right elbow into the man's left temple. This stopped him in his tracks, but to Charlie's amazement, did not knock him down. Roman entered the loo behind Kate as the turtle-necked man seized Charlie's arms from behind.

The woozy, bearded man dominated the center of the tile floor. To his left Charlie struggled against the turtleneck. To his right Roman swung a fist downward towards Kate right neck and shoulder.

Hearing his motion and sensing his distance, Kate dropped to one knee, bowing forward. Roman's blow glanced off her spine. She arched with the pain that moved her closer to the bearded brute. Angry at his being resisted by such a small woman and his being struck by a man who was not supposed to be there, the big man decided to rid himself of the woman first. His comrade would hold his other opponent while he finished her off.

Charlie stopped struggling while turtleneck tightened his grip. Now relaxed, Charlie shifted his weight subtly to his left leg. Turtleneck mirrored him, unconsciously tightening the loop of his right arm. Charlie lifted his left arm straight up from the elbow, rising out of the opponent's grip, then spinning clockwise, his right arm still entangled with his attacker's. The man tilted to his right as Charlie dropped to one knee. Turtleneck spun on one foot and looped head first toward the floor. Instead of supporting his arm as he would a practice partner's, Charlie relaxed forward and smiled as he heard the satisfying smack of a turtle falling on his back.

The door of the loo burst open, three men and one woman from the pub crowding its margins. Frozen, they saw the big man seize Kate's throat lifting her bodily toward the ceiling. Kate seized his thick wrist with both hands, swinging her left leg around his bearded neck. Her scissors did not have the desired effect. Instead of falling on his back, the brute was able to maintain both his hold and balance. She heel-kicked his face then swung the other leg over his head making a clockwise circle that twisted the giant arm. Too heavy to roll, the big man fell face first onto the tile, part of a tooth and a wad of mucous spewing from his maw, his eyes rolling back before glazing over.

A man in the doorway called back into the pub, "Call the police!"

Charlie and Kate now face Roman who begins to back away. They could see Harry helping Claire from the rear of the van.

Charlie rushed Roman, striking his chest with his left palm-heel as he reached his right palm over the gypsy's shoulder to slam the rear door. Roman bear-hugged Charlie's torso and turned to smash him against the closed door. Charlie smiled at Kate and nodded slightly to his left, taking the sudden loss of air without losing his grin. The first turtle-necked man was recovering, rising to a knee at her right side. Without taking her eyes off Charlie and Roman, Kate side-kicked Turtleneck's face back into its shell.

Still smiling, Charlie placed his right knife-hand under Roman's prominent nose, his left hand grabbing the back of Roman's slick hair. Roman arched his head and back. Slitting his legs, Charlie pushed off the door, lowered his weight and dropped Roman's groin on to his bent knee.

Charlie noticed Kate was doing her best to stay in an upright position. He grabbed her before she hit the ground. At that moment the local police came rushing in.

"Constable Jones and this is Sergeant Tom Barnes." The Constable questioned Charlie while Sergeant Barnes cuffed Roman and his three cohorts in the room. Two more policemen came in and hauled Roman and his men out the back door and into a paddy wagon in the alley. "We talked to your friends outside so why don't you tell me what happened."

Kate had recovered a little but Charlie saw that she needed to sit. "Let's go into the pub and have a seat. Kate needs to relax."

"Of course." The two officers led the way. The police had emptied the pub, although a few patrons were still milling around in front. Kate, Charlie, and Constable Jones sat down at a nearest table. Harry and Claire joined them.

"Did you know that gypsy guy?"

Claire spoke up. "He worked for my Uncle in Penzance, Billy Flynn. They were all involved in a drug bust in Scotland."

Jones stopped writing. "We heard about that." He looked at Charlie. "You were the Yank working undercover."

Charlie nodded.

"One thing puzzles me...how did they know Claire was going to be here and go to the loo where they were waiting?"

"I thought of that, too." Charlie said. "There had to be a leak somewhere."

"Not Granny's staff." Kate added quickly. "They've had all this time with Claire at Greystone to do something."

"Who served you tonight?"

Kate looked around. "I don't see him."

"Wait here." Constable Jones disappeared behind the doors into the kitchen. He returned shortly with two of his men.

"Everyone's here, except for Roger. He was your server. He also brought the drinks and wine before the meal. It would have been very easy to put something in Claire's wine glass. We're testing the food and wine now. I have a feeling the wine had something that caused Claire to go to the loo and they were waiting for her. We'll get him."

Harry told the Constable he would take Claire back to the castle. Jones nodded. Kate and Charlie proceeded to tell the Constable the whole story again. It was getting late when Kate asked if they could leave. Having already driven Harry and Claire back to Greystone, Thomas returned and was waiting outside with the Rolls.

Kate thought about the wedding the next day. "How do I look?" She turned to Charlie. She smiled at her own absurdity.

"Let's see." Charlie turned on the small light in the ceiling of the Rolls. "Hmmm...you look like a Raccoon."

"What?" Kate scrambled to find a hand mirror in the medical kit below her seat. She was horrified to see two round black eyes. Half laughing, she burst into tears.

Charlie gathered her into his arms. "You can have my back anytime, Beans."

In spite of her tears, Kate giggled. Her Dad must have told him her childhood nickname. She felt like a kid. "Really?"

"Really." He hugged her and whispered against her cheek. "I've missed you."

"Really?"

He smiled. "Yes, really."

"I missed you, too." Kate mumbled.

"What? I couldn't hear you."

"I said...I missed you!"

"A simple thank you for watching my back would be a great thing to say, Beans."

"You are insufferable."

"I know. Someone told me that just recently."

Thomas pulled up in front of the Castle and opened the door while they were bantering back and forth. Thomas opened the door. Light flooded the interior.

Kate got out just in time to see Granny leaning on her cane with a big smile.

She would love to see Kate and Charlie get together. They were perfect for each other.

Kate rushed to hug Granny. "We're okay, Granny."

"I know. Claire and Harry told me everything. Let's go inside and have some Sherry." She waved to Charlie. "Thank you for bringing my Granddaughter safely back to me."

Kate was surprised. Granny drinking Sherry or anything other than Champagne or wine! Out of the corner of her eye she saw Charlie disappear inside.

Granny led Kate into the library. Two glasses of Sherry were on a table between wing chairs flanking a roaring fire.

"I've heard everything from Harry. But are you okay? Sit down, Katie. I'm sorry about your clothes. It must have been a terrible fright for you."

"Granny, look at me and be honest. Do I look like a Raccoon?"

Granny tried not to laugh. Kate looked so serious. "I don't think I've ever looked at a Raccoon that closely, Katie. You look like the Granddaughter that I love. Tomorrow is going to be a busy day. I meant to ask Harry if they arrested all the bad guys?"

"All but Roman, Granny. They thought he'd gone back to Romania."

"Why kidnap Claire?"

"I think for the ransom."

"Harry would never let anything happen to her. Now go get some rest."

Kate hugged Granny. She hadn't realized how frail she had become. She seemed to ache in every part of her body when she got up.

When Kate got to her bedroom a hot bubble bath was waiting for her. She smiled. Granny probably had ordered her Lady's Maid to take care of her. The clothes she had been wearing were beyond repair so she dropped them in the trash bin next to the tub.

She climbed into a large claw foot tub and lay there soaking. She lay back and let the bubbles wash her hair. She could hear soft music turned on in her bedroom and a fire being lit in the massive fireplace. Granny thinks of everything, she thought with a smile. A cup of warm milk would be wonderful, she thought. She figured she had been in the tub long enough. Standing she reached for a towel and was thrilled to see a navy blue silk nightshirt under it—a nightshirt that buttoned in front? It certainly looks like a man's shirt, she thought and it came just above her knees.

She opened the door ready to climb into bed. Charlie was sitting in one of the wing chairs flanking the fire.

"I like your hair down."

"Charlie, what are you doing here?"

"I just wanted to make sure you're okay. Did you like the bubbles?"

"Did you draw the bath? And light the fire?"

"I did."

Kate clutched the front of the shirt she was wearing.

"Yep, it's mine." Charlie got up and headed for the door. "Drink your milk before it gets cold."

Before Kate could say anything he was out the door and headed down the hall to his room.

Kate sipped the warm milk and smiled. Ideas and plans swirled though her mind as she climbed into bed and snuggled under a soft comforter.

She made sure she on time for breakfast in the morning. All night long she thought about Charlie. There was something big she wanted to ask him.

TWENTY-SEVEN

Jimmy Landry was not a patient man. He wanted what he wanted when he wanted it.

He looked up the phone number for Sarah's Books in Cross Creek, Louisiana.

She answered on the second ring. Looking around she was pleased her bookshop was a success. Ladies were milling about, sitting on the overstuffed chairs and drinking cups of Louisiana's best strong coffee.

"Sarah?"

She was amazed to hear a strong male voice on the phone since this was Ladies-on-Wednesday. Right after a catered lunch, Suzie Jenkins would be doing a reading from her new book, "Women Rule. Get Out of the Way, World."

"Sarah?"

"Yes."

"This is Jimmy Landry. Do you remember me?"

"Of course, I do."

"How was the concert?"

Sarah laughed. "It was terrific but I got in a lot of trouble for not telling anyone where I was going."

"I heard. I met your friend at the airport. The one in the picture with you."

"You mean my cousin, Kate."

"Yes. I'm awful on names. Anyway Kate gave me her phone number at the airport. She was on her way to the wedding in England."

"Her cousin, Harry, is getting married."

"I lost her number. You know how it is when you're in a rush. I thought I would remember and enter it later it in my cell, but I didn't. Anyway we're supposed to meet and have dinner when she gets back. Could you do me a favor and give me her number. This time I won't lose it."

"Sure, Jimmy."

He could hear her flipping pages, probably of an old fashioned, personal phonebook.

"Here it is." Earlier Sarah had called Jock to find about the wedding. She wanted to call Kate but her business cell was out of order. Jock gave her the cell number he had given Kate. Sarah was family. This was the number Sarah gave Jimmy.

He took down the number. "Thanks, Sarah. Hey, how about lunch next time I'm in town?"

"I'd love it."

The minute he hung up, he called Kate. Usually women

fawned all over him and those were the ones he hated the most. They reminded him of his Mother who treated him like he was her lover, not her son. He shook off the thought. It made him disgusted to think of what happened when he was just a boy. He lured women with his good looks and charm. These were the women he despised.

Kate was different. She had seemed immune to his charming nature and that drove him crazy. She didn't answer the phone.

The wedding was in a few hours and Claire was in a frenzy of details. Kate rushed around seeing to the cake, the flowers, the dinner menu, and the seating placement in Granny's large dining room. Everything had to be perfect. She made sure she was seated next to Charlie.

The wedding was beautiful. Claire had chosen a dress with gold threads and pearls stitched into swirls within the cloth. Thankfully she and Harry were spared any scars from the night before.

Kate felt like a Princess in a sleeveless baby blue silk sheath. One shoulder was bare. It was plain but elegant. Silk pumps were dyed the same color to match the gown.

The wedding was small. Greystone chapel held one hundred guests and there was not a seat to spare. Neighbors and a few friends were invited.

Claire wanted her Grandfather to walk her down the aisle. He was very ill so everything had been rushed. There would be a wedding dinner afterwards in the grand dining room. Staff had been working overtime to get the silver gleaming and the crystal spotless.

The cook and kitchen staff had worked hard to make it a magnificent meal that would never be forgotten.

Kate wore sunglasses that looked strange for the evening ceremony but it made her happy. At least she didn't feel like a raccoon. Charlie smiled at her eyewear.

After a few stern looks from Granny Kate removed the sunglasses. She kept her head down hoping her hair would hide the raccoon look.

Charlie whispered close to her ear, "I like crazy girls!"

When the dancing started, Charlie held out his hand. Kate fit snugly against his chest. As Charlie waltzed her out to the terrace, it was as if they had been dancing together, forever. Kate had changed out of her tight fitting Maid of Honor gown into a dark blue velvet ball gown with tiny crystals, scattered over the bodice, that reminded her of the night sky.

"Where do you go from here?" Kate held her breath. This was the big something she wanted to ask him.

"Nowhere."

"You're not off on another adventure?"

"Nope."

"I was just wondering---"

"---wondering what?"

"Well, if you might like to come back to New Orleans with me.

We could start our own Security firm."

"We'll see."

"I have an office apartment in the Quarter."

"Your Dad told me all about Fred."

Kate blushed. "Was there anything he didn't tell you?"

"Nope."

"So?"

"I'll think about it."

Kate looked over the balustrade toward the flower filled English garden. It wasn't exactly what she wanted to hear but it was a start. One day at a time.

He never left her side for the rest of the evening. They danced, sat, talked and walked through the garden. Kate felt like she was in a fairytale but she still didn't know if she'd see him after tomorrow.

The evening's end came too soon for Kate. Harry and Claire had already left in Granny's Rolls chauffeured by Thomas. They were going to London and then to Paris, the city of lovers.

Charlie and Kate said their goodnight to Granny. Kate assured Granny she was leaving in the morning, but she planned on coming back very soon for a long visit.

He walked her to her bedroom door. "See you in the morning."

Kate smiled but she knew that was as noncommittal as it gets. She went inside and leaned against the closed door. She felt lonely. She had never felt so lost before. This was something that was totally out of her control. The thought that she would never see Charlie again was overwhelming. She climbed into bed, drew the dark green velvet curtains around her and for the first time since her Mum died, she cried.

The next morning, it was still dark outside when she made her way to the island by rowboat. She desperately wanted to talk to her Mum. She sat inside the Mausoleum crying her heart out, telling her about Charlie.

Sunlight was pouring through the stained glass windows when she returned to Greystone. She left her luggage downstairs before entering the dining room. Charlie had already served himself from the buffet.

Entering after Kate, Granny asked Watson to serve her tea in the Drawing Room. She wasn't hungry. That left Charlie and Kate alone in the spacious room.

"Eric brought our luggage to the station. I'll give you a ride."

"Thank you." Kate wasn't hungry. "I'll say goodbye to Granny."

Charlie joined her. They both thanked Granny and she asked Charlie to return soon.

"Wait here." Charlie left Kate waiting in front of Greystone.

A short time later Kate heard the roar of a motorcycle. Charlie appeared riding a huge midnight blue Harley.

Kate couldn't have been more surprised if it had been a unicorn. She laughed.

"Climb aboard!" Charlie had a big smile on his face. He looked like a young Marlon Brando with mahogany streaked dark hair, a well-worn leather jacket, a white silk shirt and jeans. She was going to miss this guy so much she wanted to get on the bike behind him, wrap her arms around him, and never stop riding.

Kate climbed aboard and Charlie sped away almost recklessly, as if trying to catch a perpetrator. He reminded her of Thunder. She wrapped her arms around him and rested her head on his back.

Charlie yelled back over his shoulder, almost drowned out by the powerful motor. "Yes."

"Yes, what?" Kate yelled back.

"You asked me a question last night on the balcony. Remember?"

"Yes? Kate held her breath. Like yes you're coming back with me?"

"Yeah, somebody's got to keep an eye on you, Beans."

She ducked her head down grateful the wind would dry her tears.

The overnight train out of Fowey left on time for London. Cabin 1A was reserved for Lady Kate. 2A was reserved for Charlie Campbell and the Harley was in the storage car.

TWENTY-EIGHT

There was a knock on her cabin door.

"Hey, Beans, are you hungry?"

Kate followed Charlie down the passageway through the lounge into the dining car. There were just a few diners left.

Kate and Charlie took a secluded table. After Charlie ordered steak for him, chicken for her, they ate their meals in silence. The server removed their plates. Charlie ordered two coffees. As soon as they were alone Kate said, "I have a question I've been dying to ask you."

"Well..." Charlie paused while their coffee arrived. The second they were alone she said, "You never did tell me. How did they transport the drugs with the fast boats?"

"The fast boats picked up drug pods resting on the bottom of the ocean. They were shaped like huge rockets with GPS. They lifted up and attached to the fast boats. The boats travelled at night. They were fast, fifty miles an hour. The boats had cooling systems on the hull to reduce the amount of heat from the machinery so they were hard to detect from heat seeking cameras. The drug pods were painted with either blue for the Pacific or green for the Caribbean.

When the fast boats were detected they released the pods that sank to the bottom of the ocean. After the fast boats were cleared by the Coast Guard the pods were picked up by other boats following their GPS signals and continue on to their destinations."

"Amazing."

Kate followed Charlie back to their cabins and said goodnight. She pulled out the cell her Dad had given her. She sat on the bed and called him but had to leave a message. "You missed a great wedding but Granny told me you were busy with a new case. Listen, Charlie is coming back with me. We're starting our own security business. I'll call you when I get back." She looked at the phone and remembered what her Dad used to say, "Look at a phone and it will ring." Sure enough, it rang.

Kate answered right away. "That was fast!" She laughed.

"I hope so! Do you remember me? Jimmy. We ran into each other at the airport. I've been trying to reach you."

"My phone's off. It's been a busy few days. How did you get this number?"

Her Dad had told her this was a secure line.

Jimmy ignored the question. "How about relaxing over dinner this coming Saturday night?"

"Jimmy, I can't. I'm actually involved with someone right now but I do appreciate your calling."

"Lucky guy." Jimmy laughed. "Another time."

"Bye, Jimmy."

As he hung up, the smile faded from his face. His eyes clouded over. She wasn't at all who he thought she was. Just like all the women he hated so much. He turned and smashed his fist through the wall. Plaster flew into the air. "That bitch!" He screamed. "She's no different." His voice dropped low and ominous, "She'll pay all right."

JUDY GARWOOD,

having been raised in New Orleans,
knows the Louisiana bayou and the
French Quarter very well.
She started writing when she was ten
years old. Being an only child,
and with both parents working long
hours, reading and writing stories
were her only entertainment.

judygarwood.com

Made in the USA
Las Vegas, NV
01 January 2023

64415775R00111